Bloody Commas

Lock Down Publications and Ca$h
Presents

Bloody Commas

A Novel by *T.J. Edwards*

Lock Down Publications
P.O. Box 1482
Pine Lake, Ga 30072-1482

First Edition October 2017
Printed in the United States of America

This is a work of fiction. Names, characters, places, and incidents either are products of the author's imagination or are used fictitiously. Any similarity to actual events or locales or persons, living or dead, is entirely coincidental.

Lock Down Publications
Like our page on Facebook: Lock Down Publications @
www.facebook.com/lockdownpublications.ldp
Cover design and layout by: **Dynasty Cover Me**
Book interior design by: **Shawn Walker**
Edited by: **Shawn Walker**

Stay Connected with Us!

Text **LOCKDOWN** to 22828 to stay up-to-date with new releases, sneak peaks, contests and more...

Thank you!

Submission Guideline.

Submit the first three chapters of your completed manuscript to ldpsubmissions@gmail.com, subject line: Your book's title. The manuscript must be in a .doc file and sent as an attachment. Document should be in Times New Roman, double spaced and in size 12 font. Also, provide your synopsis and full contact information. If sending multiple submissions, they must each be in a separate email.

Have a story but no way to send it electronically? You can still submit to LDP/Ca$h Presents. Send in the first three chapters, written or typed, of your completed manuscript to:

LDP: Submissions Dept
Po Box 1482
Pine Lake, Ga 30072

DO NOT send original manuscript. Must be a duplicate.

Provide your synopsis and a cover letter containing your full contact information.

Thanks for considering LDP and Ca$h Presents.

Dedications

This book is dedicated to my wife, who is so stomp down on all levels. You're the only true Oueen that's fit to sit beside a man like me. I'd splash a hunnit niggaz for you with no hesitation because your loyalty is real, and that's why I keep you spoiled. I love you, Mrs. Jelissa Edwards.

It's also dedicated to our mother in heaven. Mrs. Deborah Lin Edwards. Rest in Peace, Momma. Soon as I touch down in 2019, I'm buying you that grave plot that you deserve.

Rae'Jon and A'Jhani, Daddy crazy about the both of you. I know it's wild having a goon for a father, but we'll figure it out. I got the both of you for life. Soon as y'all old enough to drive, I'm putting you in somethin' foreign. Your bank accounts will stay straight. The future is yours.

To my nephews Aiden and August, uncle TJ will do all that he can to ensure y'all are straight also. I got y'all.

Acknowledgments

I pledge allegiance to the homie, Cash. I'd make them hammers bark for you. Ain't no mafucka was trying to give me and my wife a chance before you stepped in and put that cake up taking a chance on us. For that alone, I'm with you until the end, and I'll face that Reaper with you. My loyalty sealed in blood. All the commas we seeing now is because you took that chance. I ain't never met a nigga that was one hunnit, until you introduced yourself. I'ma keep this pen bleeding for you, and treat it as my hammer so I can make sure that I'm doing my part for the family.

Shawn, you are a true goddess, and it goes further than what you do for the company. You got a crazy ass brother that's coming home in 2019, so them kats out there better beware. You are the truth, my sister, and I appreciate how you hold me and my wife down. Our loyalty for you is sealed in blood, and ain't nothing we won't do for you. Love you, Goddess.

Lastly, to everybody that doubted me, thank you. A hustler needs motivation, and mine came from my own bloodline. Now watch them numbers add up.

Jehovah is real!

T.J. Edwards

Chapter 1

"*Aarrrggghhhh! Aarrrggghhhh!* Please no! Please don't kill him!" Tammy screamed, as Ajani picked Black up into the air, slamming him down on his neck. He crouched down, picking him up again, this time punching him straight in the nose, causing blood to spurt across his face.

"Bitch nigga, this shit ain't a game. Now you gon' tell me where dem birds at or I'm finna kill you, your baby and that punk ass bitch over there," he pointed at Tammy, who held their three-year-old son.

"Ajani, that's your uncle! What the fuck are you doing?" she cried.

Wham!

Rayjon took his pistol and smacked her across the face so hard with it, she flew outta the chair, dropping the little boy.

She was laid flat on her stomach, knocked out cold. A pool of blood formed around her mouth. Their little son looked up from his knees, with his hands over his ears screaming at the top of his lungs.

"Punk ass bitch!" Rayjon hollered. He got tired of her whiny ass voice. It got to irritating him, so in his mind, the only solution was to knock her the fuck out. Next, would be the little kid. Cousin or not, he didn't give a fuck. He felt no love toward him, Black nor Tammy.

"Rayjon, shut his bitch ass up, too. All that muhfuckin' noise givin' me a headache," Ajani said to his older brother, as he flung Black down into the metal chair and began taping his wrist behind his back.

"Mommy! Mommy! Peez wake up, mommy!" Lil' Black whined. He had already pissed himself. He knelt down beside his mother and ran his hand over her back. He wondered why she went to sleep after his cousin had hit her and she had an owie on her lip now. He started to cry again. This time louder than before. His wails echoed off of the walls of the sticky basement.

Rayjon scooped him up from behind, and put him into the sleeper hold. Tightening his grip every second while the boy wiggled his legs, and struggled to breathe. The more he gagged, the harder Rayjon squeezed until the little boy stopped moving all together. Then he dropped him on top of his mother. They both laid in a pile knocked out. Rayjon smile looking down on them, as Ajani tossed him the duct tape.

"This fucked up, man. Y'all ain't gotta do this shit," Black spat, as a thick rope of blood dripped of his chin. He was extremely dizzy and the room felt like it was spinning in circle. He also couldn't feel any feeling in his toes ever since Ajani dropped him on his neck. "Y'all my nephews. Cuz, we s'pose to be family."

Wham!

Ajani backed handed him with the .40 Glock. "Where dem birds at?" He wrapped his fist into Black's wife beater, and swung the toolie again.

Wham!

Splitting open his forehead, blood ran down his cheek almost immediately, and this only excited Ajani.

"*Arrrggghhh!* Nephew, awright! Awright! Nigga, you ain't gotta keep fuckin' me up." He spat out three teeth that bounced off of the ground. "Go in my son's room and move his dresser. As soon as you do that, look down and it's gon' be a hole in the bottom of the wall. Stick your finger in there and pull outward. When you do that, the whole wall will fall inward. Just look inside and them bricks gon' be right in there, cuz. Y'all can have dat shit, just leave me and my family alone," he whimpered.

"Rayjon, you heard that shit, big bro?" Ajani asked, not even taking the time to look over his shoulder at his brother. He was disgusted by how bitch-made Black really was acting.

He'd been on more than a few robberies with him where Black was the predator. During those times, he acted all hardcore and shit. Like he was really about dat life, period. Now that he was on the receiving end, he was acting like a whiny bitch, and it was pissing Ajani off.

He'd already made up his mind that he was going to kill his father's brother because, to him, that soft shit was a disgrace to the family's blood line.

"Yeah, I'll be back." Rayjon looked over at Tammy and his younger cousin once more before disappearing up the stairs that led to the main portion of the house, in search of more merchandise.

"Why y'all doin' this shit, Ajani? The fuck I do to y'all to make y'all niggaz turn on me?" Black questioned faintly, barely able to breathe, as blood continued to ooze from the slit in his forehead and spill from the place in his gums that once secured his two front teeth.

Frowning, Ajani crouched down in front of him. "You a rat, bitch nigga. My ol' man told me about the wire yo snitch ass wore while y'all conducted bidness in 'nem streets. In my eyes, you ain't nothin' but a rodent. It's time for extermination."

Black coughed up a blood loogey and attempted to spit it out, but it was so thick that it got caught on his lip and slowly crept down his chin.

"I ain't snitch on yo pops, lil' nigga. And I ain't never wear no wire," he lied.

Quiet as it was kept, he'd been working with the Feds for three months before his brother had got indicted. He was

11

warned that had he chosen not to cooperate, he would have been indicted directly after his brother was snatched up.

Caught between a rock and a hard place, he decided to take the deal. Along the way, the Feds agreed to let him keep all of the dope they'd come up with on their licks, as well as half the cash.

"Yo, Black, on some real shit, yo best bet is to take this shit like a man, 'cause you acting like a real bitch right now. We got a whole list of niggaz that need to be brought to justice. I'm hoping they all don't bitch up like you." He shook his head in disgust.

"So, you sayin' you gon' kill me anyway?" He whimpered, smelling like he was damn near ready to shit his pants. "But I just told your brother where the dope and everything at. What more do you want from me, cuz?" Tears of panic burned his cheeks.

An infuriated Ajani lunged his leg forward, *doom* kicking Black dead in his chest, causing him to flip backwards out of the chair and Ajani to land on his ass. Jumping onto his feet, Ajani walked over to Black, looking down at him with a devilish smirk, cocking his banger back. "Nigga, on my blood, if you don't quit crying like a pregnant broad, I'ma knock yo shit off yo shoulders."

Black twisted on the ground, struggling to breathe. Ajani had managed to kick the wind out of him, making him feel as if he was slowly dying. He knew that one of his ribs had to be broken.

"Uhhhh shit! Help me! Somebody, please help me," Tammy moaned, trying to get up from the ground, as nausea consumed her body. Her jaw felt like it'd been hit by a school bus.

Ajani ran over to her, yanked her up by her hair and, with all his might, slammed the barrel of his gun into her cheek ripping her skin and breaking her jaw. "You got on the stand and testified against my Pops, bitch, and shit ain't have nothing to do with you."

"Ajani, I was just doing what my husb…"

Boom!

The bullet entered her cheek, punching a chunk of her brain out of the back of her head, with Ajani still holding her by her hair. Aiming the gun at the hole that was created, he fired off another round.

Boom!

Knocking out more of her noodles. Her body jerked violently, then he let her fall to the ground.

"Punk bitch!"

Black struggled to break free. He tried his best to get his hands loose, but the duct tape was too strong. All he'd managed to do was rock his chair from side to side. "You ain't have to do that shit, nephew. What the fuck done got into you?"

Boom!

Ajani felt the jerk of his gun as it popped a bullet through the head of his little cousin. Lil' Black's brains splattered onto the concrete floor.

He then knelt down, searching for a pulse, that was faint. He was preparing to pull the trigger once more, but the pulse flat lined.

He had no remorse. The way he saw it, Black and Tammy were both snitches, which meant their son had it in his DNA to turn out just like them.

Ajani felt like he was doing the world a favor by wiping him out before he could take after his snake ass parents.

Witnessing Ajani brutally blow his son's head off, Black's worse nightmares were confirmed. It was only a matter of time before he was next on the hit list. Had he turned the Feds down, he would have only had to serve 60 months, like his brother. But his unwise decisions had cost his family their life. He felt like a straight bitch, welcoming the thought of death.

Rayjon ran down the stairs with a .45 in his right hand and a black garbage bag in his left. When he got to the bottom landing, he looked around the basement smelling the heavy aroma of gunpowder. He saw that Tammy and Black Jr. had been murdered by his brother. He wondered what they had done to set him off, but he remembered that it never took much to set Ajani off. His temper was horrible and murder was second nature to him ever since he'd witnessed their father body a nigga in front of him at the age of eight.

"Bro, did you find that shit?" Ajani asked, grabbing Black by the back of the neck.

Rayjon picked up the bag and swiftly walked over to Ajani, kneeling down and opening it. "Yeah, it's ten keys in this mafucka, pure Cola. I ain't find no money, though. And I know if this nigga got kilos in the wall, that it's money somewhere in this fuckin' house."

Ajani put the gun to his eyes and forced it harshly into the socket. "Yeah, nigga, he got a point. Where the fuck the money at?"

Black swallowed. "Any way it goes, you lil' niggaz gon' kill me, so what's the point?" He passed gas and tried to imagine what it was going to feel like dying.

He prayed it wasn't painful and that there was an actual afterlife.

In that moment, he wanted to pray, but was afraid of which God to actually pray to because he didn't want to get it wrong. He started to panic all over again.

Rayjon scrunched his face and walked over to him after pulling his lighter out of his pocket. "Oh! You *want* us to torture yo ass, huh? You wanna go out like a G?" He shook the latter up and down. "Aye, bro, grab me some lighter fluid. I saw some in the hallway right next to their barbecue grill."

Ajani nodded his head hard. "Hell yeah! That's what I'm talkin' about. Let's burn his bitch ass into dust!" He disappeared up the stairs.

Screams of terror threatened to escape Black's mouth. The last fate he wanted to experience was death by fire. He knew that would be complete torture, pain that he could not withstand.

"You know what, Black, I never liked yo bitch ass anyway. I used to peep how you looked at my mother every time my father turned his back. You a straight snake nigga and I'm gon' enjoy bodyin' yo ass."

Ajani came down the stairs and tossed the lighter fluid to Rayjon. "Drench that bitch ass nigga and let's get the fuck outta here. That nigga can either come off them chips and take two to the head or we can burn him to death and right before he dies, give him two to the head, that's up to him."

Shrugging his shoulders, Rayjon began to pour the fluid all over him until the entire bottle was emptied of its contents, then he handed it to Ajani. "Throw that in the bag and we'll get rid of it later. Even though we got gloves on, we can't be too careful." He took a step back from Black. "So, what's it gon' be, nigga?"

Black couldn't believe his fate. He had been one of the killers that trained and introduced both Rayjon and Ajani into the game alongside their father, Greed. Now, here he was on the receiving end. *Life truly was a bitch*, he thought.

He had visions on taking the easy way out with the two bullets straight to the head, but then there was the stubborn part of him that refused to bow down to lil' niggaz and give up his money. There was an intense battle going on in his mind.

"Oh, really?" Rayjon smiled with a devious grin plastered on his face. "This nigga think it's a game."

Ajani stepped forward and taped his mouth. "We finna smoke yo ass, nigga." He stood back in amazement, barely able to contain himself. Adrenaline had kicked in. He had a deep hatred for his uncle that brewed inside of him. "Kill that nigga, bro!"

Rayjon sparked his lighter, setting his uncle on fire and returned the lighter to his pocket. He could smell the cooked skin almost immediately.

"Ahhhhhhh!"

Ajani took his blunt and lit it off of the flames coming from his uncle. He heard him hollering through the tape. Then he fell on his side while the fire ate away at him.

Chapter 2

"Father in the name of Jesus, we pray that you bless this food, and that you protect us from any impurities. Thank you for blessing us with the provisions to do right for our family. Amen," Jersey said, praying over the food, as she held her sons' hands.

"Damn, Momma. You threw down, didn't you?" Ajani said, eyeing the food, placing two chicken breasts on his plate.

Rayjon elbowed him in the ribs. "Bro, watch yo mouth in front of Momma. You keep slippin' with that."

"Don't tell his ass nothing. He gon' understand when I crack him in the head with one of my skillets." She scooped some baked macaroni and cheese onto her plate, as she mugged her youngest son, who sat across the table looking like his fuckin' father.

They had the same build and everything. Ajani was just shorter than him. He was only about 5'10", whereas his father was 6'2". They were both 190 pounds, with the same dark brown eyes and dimples on each cheek that fooled most because their tempers were lethal.

"Dang, my bad, Momma. You know sometimes I be forgettin' to leave that kinda talk in them streets," he said, taking the bowl of baked macaroni and cheese from her.

It was Sunday and since the day they were born, it had been law for them to sit down at the dinner table as a family. Regardless of what was going on in their lives, they always found a way to make it home to enjoy their mother's dinners.

"Yeah well, you better get it together. Your brother shouldn't have to keep remindin' you how to behave in front of me." She put two drumsticks onto her plate, drenching them in hot sauce.

Rayjon spooned macaroni into his mouth. "If I gotta remind him every time, it don't bother me. We suppose to respect you more than anybody walking the face of this earth. That's what Pops always say."

Jersey smiled, gazing at her oldest. He was about 6'3" and couldn't have weighed more than 175 pounds, slim. While Ajani looked just like their father, Greed, Rayjon was damn near her facial twin. But as handsome as he was, she knew that her oldest was a no-nonsense killer.

"Yeah, you right, Rayjon. That's my bad, Momma. You know I respect you more than that." He felt horrible and prayed that his mother forgave him. She was his heart and there wasn't anything in the world that he wouldn't do for her.

"Do I gotta show y'all how to cook up one of them kilos or do y'all got it?" she asked, pouring red wine into her glass. "Since y'all ain't take time out to get no money, your father said y'all gotta hit the ground running right away. It's all kinds of bills coming up shortly that gotta be paid."

Rayjon shook his head. "Nall, we gon' go over to my crib as soon as we leave here and get right to business. You know we was raised better than that."

Jersey nodded her head. "That's what I thought."

Four hours later, they were sitting in front of a half brick of rock cocaine. Ajani took a Philip's screwdriver and slammed it in the middle of the brick, pulling it toward him. The cocaine cracked and slowly broke into big pieces. Ajani grabbed about 4 ounces, took his razor blade and started chopping up 20 pieces.

Rayjon leaned his head down and tooted up a thick line of cocaine that was still in its powder form. He hit both nostrils before joining Ajani at the table with his own razor blade.

He felt the high take over him immediately. His heart began to pound in his chest, and a strong sense of euphoria came over him. He started bagging up fat ass 20's, while Yo Gotti blared out of the radio's speakers.

"I'm about to snatch up August and Aiden and put them lil' niggaz down wit us. Them Blood niggaz tryna snatch up every young nigga from the hood and make 'em pledge their loyalties to 'em, but the way I see it, if we can grab a couple grimey lil' niggaz out da hood to fuck wit us, then we can lay this whole mafuckin' city down."

Rayjon curled his lip. "That dope boy shit ain't never been my thing. I rather make a mafucka suck on this hammer and take about thirty G's in less than thirty minutes than to hustle for a whole month and make halfa dat. Shit just seem ass backwards to me." He dropped another rock into a baggie, tying the end into a knot.

"I love fast money and I love slaying niggaz. I ain't got no muthafuckin' patience. And I gotta have everything toppa the line. For me, jacking niggaz is the only way." Ajani stated, bagging dubs so fast that it left his brother in awe.

Rayjon sped up his pace. Quiet as kept, the two competed with everything they did. It was something that had taken place between them ever since Ajani was two years old and Rayjon was five years old. They were exactly three years apart, sharing a birthday.

They heard keys jiggling into the lock of the front door. Both brothers scooted away from the table and upped their heat.

Ajani cocked his back after flipping it off safety. He put his back against the wall, curling his upper lip, prepared to pop a nigga dome.

Rayjon crouched down and cocked back his .44 Desert Eagle. He lightly touched the trigger, activating the red beam on top of the gun. They ran into the front room and ducked down on the side of the door, ready to body any mafucka that came through it.

Camryn turned the lock and pushed the door open, while trying to juggle the big bag of groceries that she had stupidly got placed into a brown paper bag. It felt like it was ready to bust open, plus her arms were killing her. As soon as she pushed the door all the way in, she felt an arm wrap around her neck, then she was forced into the house after dropping the bag in the doorway.

Ajani picked her up and threw her inside. Stepping through the groceries and slamming the door behind himself, he pointed the gun at her, prepared to pull the trigger. "Bitch, who the fuck is you?" he questioned.

Rayjon jumped up and ran in front of the gun. "Yo, chill, lil' bro. Dis my woman right here."

Camryn was about ready to have a heart attack. Her high yellow face had turned beet red. She was scared out of her mind. She had never had a gun pointed at her before and the snarl on the man's face that brandished it looked cold hearted. He looked like he wanted to kill her just because he could.

"Please don't kill me. I'm beggin' you," she whimpered.

"Yo, you good, Camryn. I got dis." Rayjon said, helping her get to her feet.

Ajani put his steel back at his side. "Bro, you shoulda told me that hoez got keys to yo crib and shit. I was finna blow this bitch head right off on the porch." He shook his head and pointed at the high yellow beauty. "Bitch, you lucky."

After cleaning up the groceries, Ajani grabbed the remainder of the unbagged kilo and bounced. Rayjon stepped into his bedroom and slid his pistol under the pillow, as Camryn took her place on the edge of the bed with her head down, holding the back of her neck.

Rayjon sat down beside her and moved her long curly hair out of the way, kissing her on the neck. "What's the matter, baby?"

She felt his thick lips suck her neck and immediately tingles shot down to her nipples, causing them to spike up. He licked her ear lobe before darting his tongue in and out of her ear.

"Umm, babe, what are you doing?" she asked, neglecting the fact she could no longer hide her arousal.

Rayjon placed his hand on her thick thigh and pulled it apart. He trailed his hand down to her center, tracing the lace of her panties, searching for her protruding pussy lips. That is what drove him crazy about her. She had a fat pussy attached to a small frame and it oozed honey almost instantly from his touch.

"I'm trying to hit this box. I know you ain't come all the way from the University of Southern California just for us to have a conversation." He slid his hand into her panties, inserting his middle finger deep into her hot hole.

"Mmmmm," Camryn let out a faint moan, as she arched her back and opened her legs wider, inviting him in. Her tight Prada skirt rose to her waist. "Babe, that shit yo brother did got me freaked out right now. Can we talk about that first and then you fuck me later?" she whined.

Ignoring her request, Rayjon scooped her up into his arms and threw her backward onto the bed. He climbed on top of her and ripped her panties away from her body, throwing them to the floor. "I don't want to tap into your feelings right now. I'm 'bout to kill this pussy."

"But…"

He ripped her tank top down the middle and pushed her knees to her chest, peeling away his boxers in one swift motion.

She then felt his mushroom head slice apart her slippery sex lips.

"Uhh-shit, babe, please take it eas..."

Rayjon slammed his baseball home and felt her pussy suck him in hungrily. He bit into her neck and squeezed her new set of perky twins, before beating her box in.

"Uhh-uhh! Oh shit, baby! Please slow down! Awww shit! Shit!" she moaned loudly, as her first orgasm rattled her body. She felt his thumb twerking her clitoris and his pole stuffing her repeatedly.

"Tell me who Daddy is!" Rayjon demanded, in between strokes. "Tell me who this preppy ass pussy belong to!"

"It's—it's! Ohh shit! It's yours, Rayyy! It's all yours, Daddy! Please fuck me! Fuck me harder!" Camryn cried out in ecstasy, forcing her own knees to her chest, tears visibly rolling down her cheeks. She was obsessed with that thug dick. She damn sure couldn't get it in Bel-air.

She felt him wrap his hand around her neck, slightly choking her, which brought forth her second orgasm.

Once Rayjon felt her release a second time, he flipped her onto her stomach, pulled her toward him and opened her round ass, separating her cheeks. He spit directly on her asshole, took his dick and slid it deep into her backdoor.

Camryn put her hands between her legs and started pinching her clitoris. She loved how Ray fucked her ass. He brought out her inner slut, something no other man had been able to do.

After five minutes of roughly taunting her, Rayjon felt himself reaching his peak. He grabbed a handful of her curls and release his seed deep with her channel. He slowly pulled out and rubbed his piece up and down, in between her ass cheeks.

When their session concluded, they both showered together and returned to the bed. They ate big bowls of Captain Crunch Berries and Rayjon turned on the flat screen, tuning into ESPN, making note of the scores below the screen. He was hoping that LeBron did his thing. He didn't give a fuck about nobody else in the NBA.

"I love you so much, baby," Camryn cooed, scooting closer to him, taking ahold of his dick and planting kisses on his soft head. She was in awe of him. Everything he did caused her to grow more and more obsessed with him. She was damn near hooked. She never imagined any man having that kind of effect on her.

They had met at a Laker's game, while sitting in floor seats. Instead of Rayjon paying attention to the game, or the female on his arm, he spent the entire time trying to come up with her.

She loved his persistence and his looks definitely helped!

Two months later, she felt they were going strong, and as much as she was afraid to admit it, she was in love.

"If you love me so much, you'll set up that shit I need, so that I can hit up your sister's husband's bank. I already told you I ain't gon' take more than two hundred G's. I'm tired of bringing this shit up every time, when you already know how I get down."

Camryn swallowed and sat up straight in the bed after placing her bowl of cereal on the night table, next to the lamp. Nervousness took over her and she wanted to regurgitate everything she had just eaten, all over the bed. One thing she hated was disappointing him because that would possibly cause him to kick her to the curb immediately. She didn't know what she'd do if she lost him.

"Baby, just know that I am working on it. As soon as everything falls in line, I'll let you know. I just want to ensure that there won't be any mistakes 'cause I don't want anything happening to you. I'd never be able to live with myself it something went down due to my carelessness." She fidgeted with her fingers, trying to avoid direct eye contact with him.

She didn't know the first thing about robbing a bank and she really didn't want to get involved with it in any way. Her parents were filthy rich.

For as early as she could remember, she'd always been spoiled and given the best of the best. She had a Black card in her purse and she would have let Rayjon spend every penny on it if he wanted to.

In her mind, he didn't have to rob anybody and she had hoped that sooner or later, he'd give up on the urge to do so. She wished that she'd never took him along with her to her sister's wedding. Perhaps, he would have never found out about Stanley's, her sister's husband's, profession.

"I don't need you worrying about me, shorty. I'ma gangsta, and I can hold *me* down. All you gotta do is find out when they have the most money there and a few security codes. I got the rest." He put his bowl on the dresser and popped a stick of gum into his mouth, before sliding into bed next to her, wrapping her into his arms. "Don't you love me, fa real?" he quizzed. He kissed her neck and bit into her jugular vein, licking the length of it.

She shuddered as her nipples grew hard immediately. "Baby, you know that I do, with all of my heart."

He slid his hand between her legs, peeling apart her rose petals. She moaned at the feeling of his two fingers searching for her sweet spot deep within her rosebud.

He sucked on her earlobe. "Listen to me, I'm about my muthafuckin' money and any bitch I fuck wit, gotta be about the same. You hollerin' you tryna be my main bitch, sleepin' all in my mafuckin' bed, got me eatin' yo pussy and shit, but you ain't makin' nothing happen. When you leave my crib to-day, you better get on bidness or stay yo ass in Bel-air, far away from me. Ain't no use fallin' for you if we ain't got shit in common," Rayjon whispered the last part, two fingers deep inside of her pussy.

Camryn moaned loudly as her eyes rolled to the back of her head. She couldn't afford to lose him. She was already hooked on the street thug and would do *anything* he asked of her.

As his thumb brushed across her pearl, she felt a new orgasm already taking over her. Mentally, she was gone. "Babe—I, uhhh, got you. I'll set things up. I'll do whatever, Daddy. Just please, fuck me 'til I cry." She begged between moans.

T.J. Edwards

Chapter 3

Ajani sat on the hood of his cherry red Audi S6. It was freshly candy painted, sitting on 26-inch Davins, all gold. He'd sent Aiden, his closest cousin, into the corner store to snatch up a box of blunt wraps so they could blow a quarter ounce of Bin Laden.

The sun was shining so bright, that he turned his fitted cap from the back to the front, to shield his eyes. "Man, fuck this! I'm about to snatch up my Ray Bans," he said aloud to himself, jumping off of the hood of the car.

As soon as he did, an all blue drop top '64 Impala pulled up alongside of him, with six niggaz in the car. Before he could open his mouth, five out of the six, pointed assault rifles at him that had clips hanging out of them so long, they looked like they held at least a hundred rounds each.

The passenger next to the driver spoke up. "Say, cuz, you look like you one'a dem Blood niggaz. Am I right?" he asked, mugging Ajani as if his shit stank, ready to knock his head off. The passenger hated all things red and the fact that this nigga was rolling a red Audi meant he was repping that Blood shit extra hard.

Ajani swallowed, curling his upper lip. He looked into the car at each man trying his best to remember each face. "Nigga, fuck Blood. I don't fuck wit them niggaz and they don't fuck wit me. I stand on my own two feet."

One of the niggaz in the backseat who was holding an AK47 with a blue bandana around the handle, sat up. "Yo, cuz, lemme smoke dis brim ass nigga. I know a Blood when I see one." He could already imagine what Ajani would look like with his brains splattered all over the Audi, so he wanted to be the one to do it, remembering how his brother had been slumped by the Bloodz a summer ago.

The fat nigga in the passenger's seat beside the driver, looked back at him and smiled, before focusing back toward Ajani. "I should let my lil' nigga stank you, homie. You look like one of them Blood niggaz to me."

Ajani couldn't believe they didn't give a fuck about holding him at gun point, while cars drove past. They were literally on a busy street. A city bus had already rolled pass and that didn't stop them from getting ready to splash him. He wished he had a chance to get to the Tech .9 that was under his driver's seat. He had a 50-round clip in there. If he could get to it, he would die trying to kill every nigga in that car, no matter how many bullets he inhaled.

"Say Pee Wee, get out and strip that nigga and snatch up that Audi. We can always paint that mafucka blue later," the fat nigga said, looking toward the backseat.

Pee Wee laid the AR-15 to the side of him and took a .9 millimeter out the small of his back. He jumped out of the car and slammed the barrel into Ajani's chest, as he searched his pockets, uncovering two large bundles of money and an ounce of Bin Laden.

With a snarl on his face, Ajani curled his upper lip, taking mental notes of every nigga that was in the car, including Pee Wee. He swore to himself that if those Crip niggaz allowed him to walk away alive, that he was going to see to it that any mafucka who rocked the color blue would be murdered, until he killed every one of them niggaz that was a part of him being stripped.

He prayed they'd killed him for their sake. He looked across the street and saw Aiden coming out of the store. As soon as he did, they made eye contact and Aiden nodded.

"Damn, cuz, this nigga got about 15 bands on him." Pee Wee snatched the gold rope from around his neck and put the pistol to his neck. "Nigga, open your car door so I can get in.

When you do, slide yo bitch ass over and get in the passenger seat," he ordered.

Ajani mugged him with hate. "Nigga, fuck you! Bitch nigga, if you wanna take my shit, you gon' do it on yo own 'cause I ain't helpin' you do shit. What the fuck I look like?"

Pee Wee's heart started to beat extremely fast. He was being tested. He was left with no choice. He would have to kill the nigga in broad daylight because there was no way around it. He simply could not let the nigga flex on him like that in front of his crew. That was unacceptable.

Boo-wa! Boo-wa! Boo-wa! Boo-wa!

Ajani saw the driver's head explode, sending blood and brain onto the fat nigga that sat in the passenger seat alongside of him.

Before the studs in the car could make out where the shots were coming from, Aiden was standing over their whip with two .44 Desert Eagles in his hands, finger fucking them like he was in a cowboy movie. Ajani's high yellow cousin had been smart enough to mask up first, but he knew it was him by his build, clothes, and Airmax 90s.

He shot both men in the back seat. They caught face shots and fell forward with their heads resting on the seat in front of them. The fat nigga jumped out of the car and took off running with Aiden bussing at him.

Boo-wa! Boo-wa! Boo-wa!

Ajani took the event and used it as a distraction. As Pee Wee turned around to buss at Aiden, Ajani elbowed him right in the temple, slumping him to his ass. Ajani kneed him in the face, causing his head to bounce off the concrete, knocking him out cold. Reaching under the passenger of his car, he grabbed his nickel-plated .45. He then turned to Pee Wee.

Boom! Boom! Boom!

He delivered three face shots. He nodded at Aiden before jumping into his Audi and smashed out with his left back tire rolling over Pee Wee's leg.

***

"And them bitch niggaz was Crips?" Rayjon asked, slamming a 150-round magazine into the all-black AR .33. He was ready to body some shit. He never took kindly to anybody fucking with his lil' brother. Whenever a nigga did that, he was liable to get his whole family killed including the kids.

Ajani tooted a fat line of cocaine and turned up the bottle of Ace. He felt like the niggaz had caught him slipping. There was no way he was about to take that lying down. He snorted another two lines hard. "Yeah, them niggaz was Crip. The reason they rolled down on me was because of my Audi. Mafucka gon' say I looked like a Blood." He shook his head. "If Aiden wouldn't have come tearin' shit down when he did- mann, them niggaz would have bodied me, ganked me for my stash and took the whip."

Aiden took two strong swallows from the Lean. "Fuck them niggaz, Blood. Yo, at least we knocked all they heads off. I even thought about goin' into the grocery store behind us, and bodyin' everything up in that bitch, just in case they saw some shit, but then I had to think about our mothers. What if some niggaz would have done some shit like that to them?"

Rayjon lowered his head. "Nigga, I don't even wanna think about no shit like that. A mafucka even brush Momma Jersey, I'd try to blow up the whole Los Angeles. That's my heart right there."

"That's why I ain't do it." Aiden said, lighting the blunt of Bin Laden.

He was their first cousin. Momma Jersey and his mother, Rachael, were sisters, and they were extremely close, as were he and his cousins. Aiden and his brother had recently moved over from New Jersey about four months back. His mother wanted a fresh start and to be closer to her sister.

Aiden took a long pull from the blunt. "Bitch niggaz thought it was sweet. They gotta be plugged from over on Normandy 'cuz this whole area is Bloodz and Essays. But the streets talk, so we'll find out exactly where they were plugged from and shut that shit down."

"Yeah." Rayjon agreed, taking the blunt from Aiden. "For now, we gotta fuck over Casper and his lil' crew for my ol' man. Pops say he next on the list to potentially testify against him on that secret indictment he just got word about."

"Wait, what you mean?" Ajani asked, stabbing a small pile of cocaine with his razor blade.

Rayjon blew the thick smoke into the air. "Pop said before they release him in October that they gon' try to come with another indictment. But, as long as we can knock off all of the niggaz that they got lined up to potentially testify against him, they gon' have to drop that shit because they ain't got no legs to stand on. These niggaz would be their only firepower. So, we gotta make mafuckas' hearts acapella. If you know what I mean."

Aiden took the Mach .90 off of his lap and sat it on the table. "No doubt, 'Cuz. Definitely time to make mafuckas stop breathin'. Greed is a good nigga. He ain't ever neglect to make sure my brother and I was straight at all costs. I done seen him give my mother bundles of cash at a time and never asked for shit in return. Yo, kid, ya ol' man got my loyalty. Whatever you niggaz on, I'm just tryna be down with that shit and I'm pretty sure that August is, too," he said, speaking on his little brother.

Ajani looked over to Rayjon who was rubbing his chin. He loved both of his cousins. He knew when it came down to making them guns bark, that both men were young killers with no heart.

Having Aiden and August on the team would up the ante. Not only could they knock off his father's enemy list, but they could also get their weight all the way up, by hitting a bunch of licks along the way. And since they had grown up together, and related by blood, there was a definite trust factor there. He started to imagine the possibilities.

"Nigga, if you get down with us, we gon' definitely put some bands in your pocket. We got a list of our own that's about to put us on the road to riches. I'm talking crazy commas. But, shit get real bloody because you can't have no mercy. We executin' bitchez and all."

Aiden shrugged his shoulders. "How much cake we talkin' about?" As long as the numbers were right, he didn't give a fuck about whose head they knocked off. Killing a female didn't mean nothing to him because a female could kill you just as fast as a man could.

Their Aunt Princess was the perfect example of that. Her and her husband, Taurus, were savages. Relentless killers and Princess's body count was stacked higher than his. So, in his mind, a bitch could get it, too.

"Give us a few months and you should see real close to a mill. That's not including narcotics," Rayjon reassured him, slipping the bulletproof vest over his head.

Ajani nodded in agreeance, securing his bulletproof vest into place, as well. "Nigga, we finna eat. Let's turn up!"

"Word is bond, shit finna get real bloody."

Chapter 4
Three weeks later

Ajani cut the peanut butter sandwich in half and stuffed it into the 16-year-old's mouth. "Chew up, lil' nigga. I'm finna make you eat these mafuckas until you choke or yo punk ass father tell me and my niggaz what we wanna know."

Jyrus chewed up the thick peanut butter choke sandwich and did the best he could to swallow it. Ajani had already made him eat a whole sandwich minutes before. He could barely breathe now. His windpipe felt like it was closing up. "I can't breathe, cuz. You gotta let me get something to drink," he said through a muffled voice, with tears rolling down his cheeks.

Slade wanted to leap from the chair to save his son, but he knew it wouldn't be in his best interest. Rayjon and Ajani were crazy. He had already heard about them through some of the old heads in the hood. He also knew how their father got down. He had witnessed Greed handle business on numerous occasions and the man was deadly.

Rayjon knelt down in front of him and smiled. "My Pops done brought you in our crib. You been around my momma. All along you was a snake muthafucka."

Slade felt the huge beads of sweat pop up all over his forehead. He felt like he wanted to shit himself. Especially when Aiden walked over carrying a nail gun. He pointed it directly at his face.

"Say, man, please don't do this shit, y'all. I ain't never did nothin' but respect yo father, Rayjon. I would never snitch on shit I had seen him do," he swore.

Slade was becoming hysterical. He couldn't imagine what it would feel like to get shot in the face with a nail gun.

He felt sorry for his wife's son but at the same time, he felt like it was better the son than him any day.

Jyrus couldn't breathe. He started to panic. The peanut butter was clogging his windpipe and every time he opened his mouth to try and breathe, Ajani would smack crushed saltines in it. He felt like he was drowning in mud. Every time he tried to inhale, the peanut butter would get launched further in his throat. He struggled against his binds to free himself but it was to no avail.

Ajani stood in front of him, drinking an ice-cold bottle of Dasani water. "Boy, this sho' is nice and cold, flowin' all down my throat. Mmmhmm." He shook his head after popping his lips.

Jyrus was really choking now. Shaking with his eyes wide open. His heart beating rapidly. Tears ran down his cheeks and dripped off of his chin. Suddenly, after minutes of suffering, his heart stopped and everything faded to black.

Pop!

Aiden aimed and shot the nail gun at Slade.

"Arrgghh! You muthafucka!"

Pop!

The second nail planted into Slade's face right alongside the first one, causing his blood to drip down his neck.

Pop!

The third nail entered his chin. He started shaking uncontrollably. The pain was unbearable. It felt like he had gotten stung by the biggest bumblebee in the world and its stinger had been left in his face and chin.

He started pissing on himself freely.

Rayjon slapped him on the thigh and stood up. "That's what snitch niggaz get." He grabbed him by his dreads and yanked his head backwards. "My ol' man said you got at least 80 G's of his money in this house. Where the fuck is it all at?"

He grabbed the nail gun from Aiden and pointed it right at Slade's crotch. "You got five seconds and I'ma start counting at three. So three, four..."

"Awright! Awright! All my money is in that deep freezer in there. Just dump all that shit out and it's at the bottom in Ziploc bags. It's 120 stacks. I just counted that shit."

Rayjon nodded at Ajani and he disappeared with Aiden. He took the nail gun and placed it to his knee. "So, why you turn bitch, nigga? What my ol' man ever do to you?"

Pop!

"Aarrgghh! Shit! You mutha..."

Pop!

The second nail jammed into his left knee after the first one went into his right. "I never snitch on Greed. They told me that I might have to if the indictments came down. I swear that was over a year ago and ain't nobody said shit else to me about it. I would have never said a muthafuckin' thing, though."

"Why you ain't tell him about them comin' at you on that note? What made you decide to keep that shit to yourself? Real niggaz don't get down like that."

Slade shook his head in pain. "I swear if they would have come at me again, I was gon' tell Greed. That's my family right there, man. I would never betray him under no circumstances."

Ajani came and dropped the duffel bag by Rayjon's feet. "I found the money. It was right where he said it was. I..." Ajani paused and looked over at Jyrus who was leaned forward in the chair he had been taped to, dead as a muthfucka, white foam had formed all over his mouth. His eyes wide open.

Aiden stepped behind Ajani. "Yo, let's get the fuck outta here before Brenda gets home. You know her and my mother get off work at the same time. I ain't trying to stank her ass, too. She always been one hunnit to my mother," he said, hoping they would see things his way. After all, they had already killed her only son. The teen was so disrespectful toward her, anyway, that it was almost like they did her a favor by killing him.

Ajani looked Aiden up and down and smiled. "Yo, if you ready to get up out of here like that, why don't you blow that nigga shit back?" He stood back to give him room to do what he had to do.

He took the nail gun and held it in front of Slade's face. "I never liked you anyway, kid."

Pop! Pop! Pop! Pop!

The nails entered into Slade's face again and again. Blood spurted into the air causing Rayjon and Ajani to jump backward. Slade fell out of the chair, crawling on his knees with his hands tied behind his back.

"Uhh! Uhh! I didn't even snitch, man. The Feds came at me and I ain't tell them that I was gon' do shit. I ain't say a mafuckin' thing, man." He struggled, saying his final pleads to the merciless men looking down on him with no remorse.

Ajani snatched the nail gun from Aiden and kicked Slade dead in the center of his ass. He turned over and coughed up a loogey of blood.

Ajani knelt down and put the nail gun directly to his forehead. "I hate when grown ass men cry like bitchez when the heat is on."

Pop! Pop! Pop! Pop!

He sent the nails flying out of the gun and directly into Slade's eyes. Pulling the trigger repeatedly, until Slade was as dead as a phone with no battery.

***

Averie jumped up from the couch once she heard what had to be Ajani's keys jiggling into the lock. She felt excited and could not wait to see his handsome face. He had not been home in nearly two days and she worried that he might have been laid up with another female. That didn't sit right with her.

As soon as Ajani came through the door, Averie ran and jumped into his arms. He picked her up and she wrapped her legs around his body while he held her up by her thick ass cheeks.

"Daddy, I missed you so much. You had me worried that something happened to you," she said, kissing him all over the neck.

There was no secret about it. She loved her baby daddy. He had taken her from an impossible situation and she had not needed for anything ever since then.

But, every day he stepped out in the streets, she always worried that he would be killed because she knew how he got down; or that some other broad who was more bad than her, would snatch him up. Both ways of thinking caused her to often have anxiety attacks.

"Dang, baby, you been missin' me like that? Oh, ain't that just special," he said, sucking on her juicy lips.

Averie had been his little house pussy ever since they were in the tenth grade and he snatched her away from a fuck-nigga named Game.

The nigga thought he was a pimp and had a thing for beating on females. He was at least five years older than them and back in the day, he used to patrol their high school, after it let out, snatching up any female that looked like something.

Averie was his neighbor and his sister's best friend.

Game waited until she got into the ninth grade before he snatched her up and made her his bitch. A few months later she started coming to school often beat up by him, until one day he pulled up after their school had let her out, and thought he was about to beat Averie in front of all of the other females just to make a point, when Ajani broke that shit up.

Him and Game had words, but it didn't go no further than that on that day. He told Averie that from then on, she was going to be his woman and that he would protect her from him. They'd been rocking hard ever since then.

By their senior year, she was pregnant with their son and gave birth to him the following summer.

"Daddy, I always miss you. You keep me in this house so much that all I can do is think about you all day long," she said, as he put her down. "Your son been asking about you, too."

He grabbed her into his arms and kissed her on the forehead. "Where he at?"

"He in our bed sleeping and snoring like crazy. I can't believe Jahni is only four and already he's snoring like a grown man." She laughed and shook her head. "Are you hungry?"

He watched her walk toward the kitchen with her tight biker shorts all in her ass. Averie was 5 feet even, and strapped like a stripper. She had so much ass that every time she walked it couldn't help but to jiggle. She also had the thickest thighs he had ever seen on a small female. Mix that with her caramel skin complexion, pure brown eyes and shoulder length curly hair, she was something to be seen.

Walking in the house never got old for him, because she was there. "That depends on what you cooked." He followed behind her never taking his eyes off of them ass cheeks.

Suddenly the bedroom door that was attached to the living room opened and Averie's little cousin, Stacey, stepped out wearing small red boy shorts that looked like they were painted on to her body.

Ajani hated whenever the teen was around because she made him feel some type of way. She looked like a real pretty version Stacey Dash when she was in her prime, but instead of her being slim with it, this Stacey was crazy strapped, and only 17, turning 18 in less than two weeks.

She stepped right out of the room and ran up to him wrapping her arms around his neck. "Hey, cousin, I been waiting on you to get home, so we can talk about my birthday that you know is comin' up after next week. I know you gon' go hard for me, right?" She looked up into his eyes, before kissing his cheek with her extra full lips.

Ajani felt his dick feeling some type of way. He moved her arms from around his neck and made her take a step back.

"You already know I got you. All you gotta tell me is what you really want and I'ma make it happen. How that sound?"

She squealed and started jumping up and down. "That's why I love you so much." She wrapped her arms back around his neck and kissed him on the cheek.

Averie pulled her by the arm. "Damn, bitch, get yo ass from all over my baby daddy like that. He got a whole ass woman right here." She rolled her eyes and curled her lip.

Stacey gave her a look that said she was irritated with her already. It seemed like every time she was around Ajani that woman would do anything in her power to hate on her.

She didn't understand why that was. Maybe it was because she knew she couldn't fuck with her business on no level. And she had probably caught him looking at her ass on more than one occasion.

Yeah, that's probably what it was, she figured. Her cousin was just jealous of her.

She rolled her eyes back at Averie. "Everybody know who yo baby daddy is. I ain't on shit with him. I'm just trying to make sure that he ain't gonna forget about my birthday. Damn!" She scrunched her face and closed her eyes.

Ajani's eyes had trailed down to her ass. He saw the way her ass cheeks were swallowing the material whole and that was making his manhood come from hiding. He secretly wondered what her little pussy felt like. If she could take what he would do to her. Before he could stop it from happening, his dick was starting to rise.

"He ain't gon' forget about you. That ain't in his nature. Y'all can talk about that later but for now I wanna put some food in my man's stomach. Is that okay with you, baby?" she asked, looking pass Stacey.

Ajani nodded. "Yeah, baby, go make me a plate and put it in the microwave. Let me holler at her real quick in here and I'll be ready to eat in a minute."

Averie smiled. "Okay, Daddy. Then after you eat you can spend some time with your son."

Ajani nodded and grabbed Stacey by the arm. "No doubt, ma. First let me holla at her about disrespectin' you in front of me like that."

Stacey started to protest, but he grabbed her by the arm and took her right back into the room, closing the door behind them. As soon as it was closed, he walked into her face and she kissed his lips hungrily. She felt him slide his hand into her boy shorts. His fingers separated her pussy lips before his middle finger entered her, causing her to open her thick thighs wider.

"Ummm! Shit!"

He sucked on her lips and then bit her neck. "You know I'm about to beat this pussy up on yo birthday, right? I'm gon' show you what this grown dick like, then I'ma put you down in my nigga club because you ready to get that paper for

Daddy. You know that, right?" He stuffed two fingers up her and twirled his thumb around her clitoris.

She closed her eyes and opened her mouth wide. "Uhh! Shit, Daddy! I'll do whatever you say. You just gotta fuck me like you promised on my birthday. I'll do anything for this dick." She reached between them and grabbed his pole, feeling its thickness. "Please, can I see it again? I ain't seen it in a few days."

He worked two fingers in and out of her while her eyes rolled into the back of her head. Her boy shorts were now around her thighs. Bald pussy exposed and dripping sex juices. He sped up the pace and sucked hard on her neck.

"You gon' see it on yo birthday. You just gotta be a good girl for Daddy until then, and you gotta respect my baby momma. You understand me?"

Stacey was humping into his hand and playing with her own breasts. She pulled her tank top up and started pulling on her nipples while he finger-fucked her into oblivion. She would do anything that Ajani said with no problem. He had her hooked.

Chapter 5

Greed dropped down and did another 100 pushups straight. He had sweat dripping off of his bald head, yet the wind felt good on his back. After the hundredth one, he stood up and dusted off his hands.

"Say, Chief, it look like them Arab mafuckas on they way over here," said Lox, as he put his hand under his shirt close to the ready-made shank with the 8 inch blade. "You want me to start poking shit as soon as they cross the line of dip bars?"

Greed turned to see what he was looking at. Sure enough, it had to be about ten Arabs on the way over to their section, which was uncharacteristic of the bunch. The only time they mingled with the Blacks were during Islamic service. Other than that, everybody stayed with their own race.

Greed felt the heavy shank in his draws. It had a 10-inch ridged blade and he was ready to do some damage with it. "Just stay on point, brah. If these mafuckas looking like they ready to pull one, then go for what you know. I'll give you a signal if I want you to start bodying shit."

Lox nodded. "Awright, yo, but what the signal gone be?" he asked, looking out into the rec yard as the Arabs got closer to them.

"You'll see me slam my shit into the first mafucka's neck. That'll be the signal," he laughed.

Kabir slowly walked over to the ripped-up muscle bound black man. He couldn't help swallowing and silently prayed to Allah that nothing jumped off with the Blacks. He needed to speak with Greed. He knew he was the right man for the jobs he needed taken care of.

As soon as he got to the dip bars, three black men jumped up with shanks out. One with dreads so long that they touched the middle of his back. He looked like he lifted weights all day long even in his sleep. His skin was as black as a shadow. "Say, homie, what the fuck y'all doing on our side of the rec field?" Killa asked, with his face scrunched up.

Lox took a step toward them. "Yeah, this ain't the Temple."

He was hoping some shit popped off so he could kill a few of the Arabs. He personally didn't like nothing or nobody that he didn't know nothing about. They freaked him out and because they did, he wanted to kill them.

Kabir held up his hands. "My brothers, we come in peace. I only wish to talk to Greed. It is a matter of extreme finances. We pose no threat to you or your men. That I can assure you."

Lox stepped forward and pulled out his shank. It looked like a mini sword. "You mafuckas already know that if you wanna holler at our chief that you request that shit in writing and get it to his Generals. That's y'all problem. You mafuckas don't respect this Nation bidness."

Killa pulled out his shank ready to get down. "What you sayin', Lox, we about to send this bitch up?" He stepped toward the Arabs and every last one of them pulled out their shanks.

It turned out that the foreign men were down to shed blood if they had to, as well.

Seeing this, Kabir stepped forward, keeping a safe distance and looked over Killa's shoulder. "Greed, I'm talkin' more than a million dollars here. Please just hear me out."

Greed gave the nod to his hitters. "Yo, let him come through but the rest of them mafuckas gotta stay back there. This ain't got shit to do with them."

After getting everything squared away. Greed led Kabir to the bleachers, where both men took a seat. "First let me thank you for the interview on such short notice. I understand that you are a very busy man and well respected. I don't mean any disrespect toward you and the way I conducted things. With that being said, I need your services."

"My services? What services are those?" he asked, catching a whiff of the Arab man and not liking his scent. He smelled like a weird kind of musk cologne that wasn't sitting right with his stomach.

"I'm just going to come out with it. There are a bunch of rats that I need taken care of before they go in front of the grand jury. The sooner you can have them knocked off, the better. I'm set to go in front of the grand jury, myself, in a month. If there are no witnesses to stand against me I will be a free man. I am set to be deported no matter what, but back in Saudi Arabia, I am nearly a prince. I will not forget about you, even after the million-dollar payout."

Greed rubbed his chin. "I'll need contact information of everybody."

"That won't be a problem. I'll get them to you by the morning."

"I want a hundred thousand dollars up front sent to a certain off shore account and a copy of your visitor's list."

Kabir swallowed. "The money is as good as sent. But why do you need a copy of my visitor's list?"

"Because if you fuck me over in any way, well, let's just say you hold up your end of things and I'll do likewise. Real men never make threats."

As fearful as Kabir was to get in involved with Greed, he knew that he had to. He came highly recommended and he was the only one that could prevent him from spending the rest of his life in a federal prison.

He stood up and extended his hand. "I'll meet you at the janitor's closet right before breakfast. There, we'll exchange everything that we need to in order to make this a success."

***

Greed watched Jersey saunter over to his visiting table with her Burberry skirt so short that damn near all of her caramel thighs were exposed.

One thing he loved about her was how pigeon toed and bow legged she really was. There was no sexier woman on the face of the earth to him than his wife. He would body a mafucka over her in a heartbeat and had already twice before, one time being her own father.

As soon as Jersey got into his huge arms, she felt him wrap them around her, then she was lifted into the air like a little baby.

Only being 5 feet 4 inches and weighing no more than 125 pounds compared to his 6 feet 2-inch frame, carrying 210 pounds of weight. He had no trouble hoisting her into the air.

Every time he did it, she always felt like a little girl again. She had been with Greed ever since she was 16 years old and her love for him had not died in the least bit.

"Damn, baby girl, you smell so good. I almost forgot how soft and perfect this body was," he said, sniffing her up before sucking all over her neck.

Jersey closed her eyes and almost wanted to cry. She wanted him home. She hated that part of the game. The part where prison was one of the equations that came along with everything else.

He ended with palming her ass. As she sat down across from him, she crossed her legs, causing her skirt to rise further up on her thighs. "Our boys been out there killing shit left and right."

Greed nodded his head. "I told them what needed to be done and I raised them to respect and honor me and you."

"I know that and that they have been. Brenda taking it hard, though," she said in a soft voice. "Hold on, baby, I'll be right back." That microwave finally opened up. She watched the heavy-set sister walk away with an arm full of food.

She had been irritated when she'd first gotten into the prison and saw that one of the two microwaves was broken. The only other one was being occupied by a Mexican sister that looked like she bought one of everything out of the machine.

Jersey knew she wasn't about to wait on her to get done. She always liked to have her husband's food done by the time he got to the visiting center but this day, because of the Mexican woman, she had dropped the ball and that made her feel like a horrible wife.

Greed looked around the visiting room while she went and whipped up their vending machine food.

As usual it was packed. *Baby Momma Central.* There were so many kids running around that his nerves started to bother him. He loved his own boys, but he wasn't for tolerating other people's kids. It seemed like children always found a way to wipe something nasty on him. And the way most of the visitors were set up, they were spending more time sucking face and flirting with one another that they barely paid any attention at all to their lil' ones. He just hoped that none of them bothered him. He wasn't opposed to pushin' one down.

Luckily, Jersey showed up ten minutes later and sat his food down in front of him. She even placed a napkin on his lap, before kissing him on the cheek. "I got everything I know you like, baby. I gotta watch my man eat. I can't have you coming out all skinny and shit," she said seriously.

She had never seen him small and never wanted too. She felt like if he ever started to lose weight that that meant she wasn't doing her job.

"Now what was you saying about Brenda?" he asked.

She lowered her head. "She's taking Jyrus' death pretty hard. His funeral was yesterday and she passed out about five times." She shook her head. "It was so sad. I felt real bad hugging her knowing what really took place with my babies."

Greed shrugged his shoulders. "That's the price she had to pay for fuckin' with a bitch nigga. That's how the game go. I been telling you this shit ever since we were kids. You can't have no emotions at all, outside of our family because on any given day, whomever you care about; we might have to body their ass, and then what?"

He sent his prayers up to Jehovah, before taking a bite of his cheeseburger. "She lucky she still alive, and the only reason she is, *is* because of you."

Jersey nodded knowingly. "I know, baby. But let's not talk about that anymore because I can tell its bothering you some. I want this to be a good visit because I miss you." She leaned across the table and kissed his cheek.

"I'm sending you a hunnit bands out this week. I need you to verify our Swiss account on Friday. As soon as that sum drop in there, I need you to transfer it to the Caymans. That's very important."

She nodded, wanting to ask more question but knowing how her husband got down, she decided against it.

Some little girl with chocolate all over her face made her walk over to her with her hands out like Frankenstein.

Jersey jumped up immediately and pointed down at her. "Uh, somebody's baby is over here." She looked around the visiting room until she located a short Puerto Rican woman. The woman shot up from her seat. She ran and picked up the little girl.

"I'm so sorry about that," she said, carrying the two-year-old away with her screaming at the top of her lungs.

Greed started laughing. "Yo, you jumped up quick as hell. You wasn't tryin' to let that lil' girl get nothing on that Burberry, huh?" He took a long swallow from his pink lemonade.

Jersey gave him a serious face. "I feel just like you feel when it comes to other people's kids. I don't like them puttin' their dirty hands all over me like that. Shit, I love our boys but when they were little that used to drive me crazy. It seemed like they knew how to track down everything gross, then they would transfer it to me." She rolled her eyes. "Then that lil' girl had chocolate all over her lil' face and hands. I came here to look my best for you."

"Baby, ain't no other woman in this world more beautiful to me than you are. Them clothes don't make you. You make Burberry look good."

Jersey felt herself blush. After all those years, Greed always knew what to say to her to make her feel like the most special woman in the world.

"Thank you, baby." She reached across the table and rubbed his handsome face.

"I need you to kill Brenda," he said this and took another bite out of his cheeseburger.

Jersey felt her heart stop. She had to be sure that she heard him correctly. "Baby, what did you say?"

He continued to chew his food. "It's only a matter of time before she put the pieces of the puzzle together. I can't have that. So, since I had our boys spare her for you, I want you to kill her on your Bloody shit. Ain't nobody bigger than this family, including her and your feelings toward her."

Jersey took a deep breath and exhaled loudly. She felt her throat go dry and her heart was beating faster than it ever had before. She would do anything for their family and over the years her husband had made her prove that time and time again. But what he was asking this time was so extreme.

Brenda had been her best friend ever since she had moved from New Jersey. The woman was the first to embrace her in California and when she couldn't find her way around, Brenda was the one to show her the ropes. To kill her would be almost impossible. She was her only true friend.

Greed wiped his face on a napkin. "You know I really don't like when you're that far in your head. That tells me that you done developed way too much for somebody that ain't of our family. So you know what I'ma do, I'm gon' take the reins out of your hands and handle her myself." He leaned forward and looked her over closely.

That was one of the things that he hated about being locked away from his family. He couldn't keep them on the straight path. With him absent, it caused them to form emotional bonds with outsiders, bonds that could prove to be destructive to their way of life.

He knew that requesting for her to kill Brenda would be a hell of a task, but it was necessary because he also knew that by him being away, Brenda was the one and only person his wife would turn to for moral support. Support that he didn't want her seeking from anyone else.

The first rule to the game when it came to building a strong family empire was to always make sure that the family never sought outsiders for any form of support. Everything had to come internally.

Jersey saw the look on her husband's face and to her it read disappointment. It was a look that killed her soul.

"Baby, if that's what you want me to do, then I will. I'll handle business just like you taught me to because like you said, neither one of us is bigger than this family. I sense that you view her as a threat and I have never questioned your judgement so therefore she gotta go," she swallowed, trying to imagine in her head how she would make it all happen.

Then, she continued. "One thing I will say is that I do care about her and killing her is going to feel like I am killing my own sister."

Greed reached across the table and grabbed her small hand. "It's supposed to."

T.J. Edwards

Chapter 6

"That's four ounces at six hundred apiece, my nigga, so that's twenty-four hundred dollars all together," Rayjon said, as he dropped the dope into Lil' Mike's lap, looking him over closely.

The teenager took the dope and put it in his back pack and came out of his pocket with a knot of money, all hundreds. He counted out 24 big faces and handed them to Rayjon. "It ain't gon' take me long to pop this shit. I like it 'cause it's all powder, so I can rock my shit up on my own. So I'ma take this foe and rock all afternoon and I should be getting back up wit you later on tonight for 8." He shook up with him and stepped off the back porch.

Rayjon was getting ready to close the back door when a green Lexus pulled into the back of his crib. He watched Lacey get out of the car once it came to a stop.

Lacey was an Asian and Black chick that he'd went to high school with. Even back then, she was hustling. She was fine as a muthafucka. Always fitted and only fucked with females.

As soon as they made eye contact, she threw her hands into the air. He waved her over. He'd heard she had gotten a modeling contract with Cover Girl cosmetics. He wondered why she was pulling up at his crib, especially unannounced.

"Damn, nigga, I'm surprised I caught yo ass up this early in the morning." She stepped on to the porch and gave him a hug, feeling the hard Kevlar vest that protected his chest.

He squeezed her so tight that the handle of his banger poked her in the stomach.

She smelled like Chanel. He always had a thing for females that rocked those expensive scents. It told him that they took care of themselves. If a woman would go all out to spend money on the way she smelled, it had to mean that she kept herself all the way up.

He hugged her tightly and kissed her on the neck, knowing that it was the furthest she would allow him to go. "Why you ain't hit my phone before you strolled through here? You lucky I ain't closed the door in your face and told you to keep it moving."

She stepped out of his embrace and gave him a crazy look. "Nigga, you ever do me like that and I swear you gone need more than this funky vest to stop me from killing you. I been your girl since freshman year. I got *carte blanche* over every other muhfucka you dealin' with. Never forget that." She kissed him on the cheek.

"Anyway, what's good? Why you ain't hit me up first?" He smiled.

"One of my bitchez broke my phone on some jealous shit. I ain't got your information no more. Luckily, I remembered how to navigate over this way. I felt the only way I was gon' be able to catch you today was if I came through early. I see I was right."

Rayjon nodded, trying his best to not let the scent of her get to him. It didn't help that she was so fucking fine. He hated that she only messed with females because if she didn't, he'd be trying to keep her in the house. She was definitely trophy status. He could see himself coming home to somebody like her after trapping all day.

"So what's up?" he managed to ask.

"I need at least six zips. I got a bunch of these modeling hoez that's trying to get down wit me. All they do is snort coke. That's basically their breakfast, lunch and dinner."

"Oh yeah?" His interest was piqued.

"Yep." Lacey nodded her head. "Ever since I been work-ing at this new agency, I can't keep no steady connect because

I'm always flying out of the country and soon as I get back, whoever I was fucking with has either moved or been popped off. So I need a steady connect and I know you know where to direct me."

He looked over her shoulder to make sure nobody else was coming up to his door. "Awright, I'ma fuck wit you. Come on inside." He moved out of the way, but just a little.

Lacey would have to rub against him to get by so that was like he hit the jackpot because she chose to enter with her back to him, rubbing that perfectly rounded ass against his growing dick print.

Lacey knew what he wanted and she decided to give it to him. Besides, even though she only preferred pussy, from time to time she liked to feel a nice sized dick rubbing up against her. It let her know she not only had the females locked down, but also the men.

As she slowly squeezed by him, she made it a point to poke her ass out to feel him as best she could.

Rayjon was seconds away from snatching her lil' ass up and bringing her over to the men's side of things. It took all of his willpower to not do so. He wrapped her in his arms and kissed her on the neck with her ass still in his lap.

"You better stop playing wit me. You know I'll kill this shit if you gave me that chance." He ran his hands up her hips and all the way to her titties squeezing the B cups through her Fendi top.

When his thumbs rubbed across her erect nipples, she moaned and pushed her ass back further into him. "You been telling me that since school, so I already know. But I only fuck wit pussy. What you got between yo legs definitely ain't that." She pushed his hands off of her and walked further into his crib.

There was a whole kilo of dope on the table, along with a box of sandwich bags.

Rayjon sat down in one of the chairs and invited her to do the same. He spaced two nice sized lines and prepared them to be tooted up. He took a straw and snorted the first line hard.

"May I?" Lacey asked, already eyeing the candy. She knew that it had to be that *sauce* if he was associated with it.

He waved her off. "Stop playing wit me, shorty. You ain't even gotta ask." He leaned down and tooted the last line and sat back in his chair with his heart racing. The dope took over him immediately. He felt energized, excited and like it was time to get money.

Lacey spaced four thin lines and took them two to each nostril. As soon as she finished, she laid back in her chair with nipples so hard they felt like they wanted to pop off of her titties. That was the only down side to her indulging, because whenever she did, the drug always made her extremely horny. She prayed that Rayjon didn't try anything with her while she was in this state because she would make a huge mistake.

He weighed a total of ten ounces on the scale and shuffled it into a Ziploc for her. "This ten zips right here. How much money you bring wit you?" he asked, looking over her flawless face.

He definitely didn't miss them thick nipples sticking through her top either. He got hard immediately and knew he was gon' have to slay something before he got on the grind.

Lacey rubbed her thighs together and tried to think about something other than him bending her over the table and fucking her until she came all over him screaming how much she missed dick. She imagined he would fuck her so hard that she wouldn't be able to stand up and that caused her to leak into her panties.

Pushing this unexpected thought from her mind, she asked about business. "What you gon' charge me?"

"These run for 6 apiece. I'm giving you ten so that's 6 bands."

"Aiight, that's cool. But you know I don't fuck wit cash. I'll just send it to your pay pal account. Give me the info." She pulled out her new phone and as he gave her the information, she handled the business.

The whole time Rayjon eyed her closely. Her mannerisms were so feminine. Her nails and toes were done and she had a nice lil' elegance about herself.

As she got up to leave with the dope, he stood up as well. "Lacey, on some real shit, I ain't finna let you leave right now without giving me some of that pussy. We been knowing each other way too long for you to be holding that shit from me." He walked up on her and made her walk backwards until her back hit the wall and there was no escape.

She moaned deep within her throat. *Damn, I knew I shouldn't have come in here and I knew I shouldn't have hit them last two lines.*

Her body was screaming for relief, and quiet as it was kept, she had always been crazily attracted to Rayjon. But she held onto her game face.

"Boy, stop playing wit me. You know I don't get down like this." But she didn't stop him when his hand went up her skirt and she felt him rubbing her pussy lips through her laced panties.

Rayjon rubbed his fingers together after feeling the heavy moisture on them. There was no denying that Lacey was wet as a muthafucka. He put his hand in her panties and played over her naked lips.

Fuck! Her entire pussy was drenched in her own juices.

She pushed him on the chest with a light force. "No! This ain't going down like that, bro." She tried to push him away from her, but not with much sincerity.

Rayjon crashed her into the wall and pinned her with his forehead against hers. "If this how you want me to hit this shit, then so be it." He pulled her down to the floor and got between her shapely legs, ripping her panties away from her, causing her to moan.

As soon as they were gone, he pulled his dick out, already hard and pulsating like an angry snake on steroids. He put the fat head to her opening and it was like the heat from her box was searing him.

Lacey opened her legs wider, as she felt him entering her pussy. "So, you just going to rape me, Rayjon? Huh? Is this what you really wanna do?"

He bit into her neck and slammed his dick home until his balls slapped against her ass cheeks. "Hell yeah!"

Lacey came as soon as he filled her up. She felt so embarrassed. "Uhhhh! Oh shit! Ummm hmmm, nigga!" She opened her legs wider and she began to shake, digging her nails into his back.

Rayjon was in a zone. He was pulling all the way back and slamming his dick into her at full speed, hitting bottom. Her pussy was good, wet and snug. It felt like she was milking him for all he was worth and he was trying to kill her pussy.

"I'm finna make you switch the game up!" he growled, with veins coming into his neck.

Lacey felt like she was being nailed to the floor. His dick ran in and out of her so fast she couldn't keep up. It felt so good that she wanted to cry.

Every time he'd smash into her, his stomach would cause her clit to tweak. Before Lacey knew it, she started to pinch her own clitoris, while his big pole dug her out.

Rayjon tossed her legs on to his shoulders and closed his eyes. He couldn't believe he was fucking Lacey. He had to make the best of it. His father always told him that every now and then a lesbian craved dick.

"If one was to ever choose you to be that dick you make sure you wear her ass out because you will become her loyal piece. And that's something every man can be proud of."

So he drove into her with anger and pure lust while she screamed under him with tears rolling down her cheeks.

***

"This is everything that you requested of me. I have marked the hits down in order as I want them taken care of. The money that you asked up front will be wired into your account before breakfast starts. Also, this is a cell phone that can't be traced. You can use it to do your thing. If there is anything else that you need, please let me know," said Kabir, looking up at the beast of a man.

Greed took everything the man handed to him with the exception of the phone. He handed him the information for the wire transfer.

"It's just one other thing that I need from you. I gotta know why you need me to handle all of this shit for you if you got connects everywhere? It don't seem like it took you that much of an effort to come up with all of this. So why not use some international hitman? Why me?" He looked him over very closely as he went over everything in his head. The whole thing seemed to be a little fishy.

Kabir looked over his shoulder to make sure nobody was coming down the hallway before replying. "You came highly recommended by those up top. Some are very familiar with your body of work with the Ski Mask Cartel. A lot of people hate you because of it, but not Don Deniro."

As soon as Greed heard Don's name, all he could do was nod his head. "Awright, man. Like I said before, you just hold up your end and I'll make sure that mine is taken care of. Keep updates on this list, very shortly it's going to disappear."

Kabir wanted to hug the man, but he knew that would be ill advised. In his culture it was obligatory, but in America it was considered weak. So he offered a handshake.

Greed wasn't the one for shaking hands. He really didn't like other men, especially touching the, and he was an extreme germaphobe. He simply balled his hand into a fist and bumped them with the man.

***

Lacey, felt Rayjon pull out of her. As his dick was leaving her wetness, she began to feel so empty, like she had betrayed her people and her beliefs. Even though she had to admit that it felt so good, it was leaving a bad after taste in her mouth that slightly bothered her.

She laid on her back for a few moments longer with her legs wide open. Rayjon got on his knees and rubbed her fat juice box. He couldn't believe how meaty it actually was. He had never seen a pussy so fat.

"Ma, you strapped as hell down here. I ain't never know you was holding like this," he complimented, biting into her thigh.

Lacey sat up and shook her head. "Damn, I feel crazy." She got all the way up and found her skirt, stepping into it. She picked her ripped panties up and maintained her silence.

Rayjon, detecting that something was wrong, got up and tried to put his arm around her, but she pushed him away.

"What's the matter?" He grabbed her arm and made her face him.

"Let me go, Rayjon. I feel like shit right now. I don't know what I was thinking," she whimpered.

"Thinking?" he frowned. "Man, shorty, you been my nigga since forever. What, you think because you gave me the pussy that I'ma flex on you or somethin'?"

She shook her head. "Nall, it's not that. I just don't want our relationship to change. You're the only man that keep shit gangsta wit me. I love that you treat me like I'm one of the guys but at the same time you, make sure I'm straight. That's what I need. I don't want that to change."

He pulled her into his arms and kissed her on the forehead. "You always gon' be my nigga. And I'ma hold you down, no matter what. Just 'cause we fucked don't mean shit gotta change. The only thing I hope change is that we actually fuck on a regular basis now or at least whenever you get that craving for dick, I'm the one you sit on."

She laughed. "Yeah, I knew you was gon' find a way to throw something like that into the air." She kissed his chest and rubbed all over his stomach. "On some real shit, I been feeling you like that, though. You could've hit this pussy a long time ago if you just took it."

Rayjon felt a tingle go through him.

It ain't nothing like a female that loved getting that pussy took by the right nigga, he thought.

He reached down and cuffed her ass and pulled her more firmly into him. "Had I known that, I would've took this shit in the ninth grade instead of going home and pulling on this dick with your image in my head."

"You used to jack off thinking about me, fa real?" Lacey giggled.

"Hell yeah, because even when we were younger, your nipples used to always show through your tops and you had a lil' round ass that used to drive me crazy."

Lacey smiled. "Well, you gotta keep in mind that we still niggaz and I still like pussy. If it come down to me needing some dick, then I'm gon' come to my protector and get what I need. Deal?" she asked, looking up at him.

He kissed her on the forehead. "Yeah, that sound like a plan."

Chapter 7

"Girl I'm so glad you invited me over here. I been going crazy in that house all by myself. It seem like everywhere I turn it reminds me of one of my men," said Brenda, taking the glass of Chardonnay from Jersey.

Jersey waved her off. "You my girl and you should already know that if anybody gon' hold you down it's going to be me. We been stomp down ever since I left the East coast."

Brenda took a sip of the wine and nodded her head. "You always tell me that I'm more of a sister to you then Rachael is. I hope that's the truth because I do try to be." She took another sip and started dancing from the waist up. "This that shit right here."

Jersey swallowed hard. She knew tonight was the night she had to handle business and it was fucking with her a little bit. Every time she looked at her friend, her heart broke a little bit.

She was trying her best to not shed a tear. "Girl, you want me to put on some of that Trey Songz so we can fall back and just vibe?"

"Bitch, you already know." Brenda put a thick blunt on the table, followed by a mini Ziploc of Loud. "I got some shit from Long Beach that finna have yo ass tripping. This the best shit they got out in Cali right now."

She took the blunt off of the table and lit it, inhaling deeply before blowin' the smoke out slowly. To her, there wasn't nothing like a smooth flow. Just because the weed didn't hurt her chest didn't mean that it wasn't the bomb.

Jersey started the music and took a deep breath to calm her nerves. She was trying to go over their whole history in her mind to try to recall some small form of a betrayal that would motivate her to do what she needed to do, but she could not come up with anything.

The entire time they had been friends, Brenda had always held her down and treated her better than anybody outside of her immediate family. It honestly pained her to do what she was getting ready to do.

"Girl, what's taking yo ass so long in there? I hear the music, now come on in here and sit back. Groove wit me, baby." She smiled and licked her lips, before picking up a glass of wine. "I'm already buzzing. And for the moment, I ain't got no worries."

***

Ajani threw stacks after stacks of money into the black garbage bag while Aiden kept the huge shotgun stuffed down Pit's throat so far that he had already threw up twice over the barrel.

Ajani loved the way his cousin got down. He always seemed to bring that East Coast mentality to every lick that they hit. It made things so much easier.

He finished emptying out of the safe and stood up, looking around the living room at the destruction they had caused all because Lando wanted to play around with the location of the money.

He shook his head with mock pity. "Yo, Lando, on some real shit, I wasn't even gon' body you until you made us go through all of this," sighed Ajani, taking his mask off. "You see all this sweat on my forehead and shit. This is what got you murdered. Not the lick within itself, but all because you chose to make a nigga get all musty and shit!"

Lando tried to explain himself but the barrel was stuck so far down his throat that he could barely breathe. He didn't understand how he had got caught slipping. How did they make it into his garage and most importantly, why was Greed sending his kid to kill him after he had already vowed to not take the stand against him.

Aiden leveled the shotgun. "Yo, kid, am I blowing this nigga shit back yet or not? My arm getting tired." He could already imagine how Lando's brains were going to jump out the back of his head. It was exciting him to even think about it.

He had watched Lando hit on his mother on some aggressive shit on more than one occasion. She always turned his ass down and yet he pursued her even still.

Ajani ordered his cousin to take a step back. "Let me hear what this fuck nigga gotta say before you splash him."

Aiden nodded and took the barrel out of Lando's mouth but kept it pressed so firmly against his forehead that it broke the skin.

A small trickle of blood formed around where the steel met brown skin.

"Speak, nigga!"

"Ajani, I swear I ain't did nothing for your father to order my hit. I been one hundred percent loyal to him and the Cartel. I know this shit got something to do with the Feds, but I'm telling you I was never finna roll over on the homey. That's on my kids, man."

Ajani wiped the sweat from his brow and transferred it to his shirt. He really didn't give a fuck what Lando was talking about because once his father had already told him that he was to never let a vic see his face without killing them. Mix that with the fact that his orders were to annihilate anybody his father sent him to, the cards really wasn't in Lando's favor.

Ajani had promised he wouldn't kill him but he never said that *Aiden* wouldn't. Smirking, he said, "You know, Lando, I hate when a mafucka get to cryin' and actin' like a bitch when it come to this gangsta shit. When a mafucka got you how we got you, you gotta take this shit on the chin because ain't no out, other than a black out. So, in honor of yo bitch and kids, my nigga, man the fuck up and go out like a gangsta."

Lando started to panic. "Like a gangsta! I ain't did shit. Ain't no reason to die if I ain't did nothin' to deserve death. I ain't never been a snitch. I would have never rolled over on Greed. That's my nigga and he always have been. I helped raise you and your brother, lil' homey," he pleaded.

"You can save that shit." Ajani wasn't trying to hear that noise, but Lando wasn't giving up.

"It's been plenty of times your father was under the gun and I saved that nigga's life. That's gotta count for somethin'." Ajani started to take what he was saying into consideration even though his father had never told him anything like that.

He knew his father was a complete savage back in the day and his Ski Mask Cartel was relentless. Lando had ran with him since they were teenagers back in Chicago. He even moved out West with Ajani's pops because they were so close and they depended on each other.

Ajani was met with a dilemma. "Fuck it. You know what, Lando? I'ma…"

Boo-wa!

Lando's head jerked backward suddenly, almost ripping itself away from his neck. Large pieces of brain fragments and blood splashed across the walls. He fell on to his side with a hole in his face so big it caused what his skull kept in place to ooze out into the carpet in a bloody mess.

Ajani jumped back having been caught off guard. He looked over at Aiden, who held the smoking shotgun up against his shoulder.

Aiden answered the unspoken question that was frozen on his cousin's tongue. "Fuck that nigga, man. All them mafuckin' words was gettin' on my nerves, kid."

***

"Bitch, you know you lyin' like a muthafucka. I saw how you looked at him quit a few times. You might not have acted on nothin', but you definitely did some lustin'," she said, taking another pull on the blunt and passing it to Jersey.

"I swear on my kids that ever since I been with Greed, I ain't never desired another man. He fills me completely up. I mean that with all of my heart." She started to imagine him in her mind's eye and that caused her to become a little sick. She missed her husband and prayed he would be coming home soon.

Brenda swallowed. Suddenly she was missing Slade and her son. She tried her best to change the subject. "So, when is Greed coming home anyway?"

Jersey exhaled loudly. "Soon enough. Long as they don't have enough supporting evidence to charge him with anything new, then he should be home in less than twenty months. Fingers crossed of course." She took the blunt from Brenda and inhaled the putrid smoke.

Brenda curled her upper lip. "Lucky bitch." She sat back on the couch after rolling her eyes.

She felt like Jersey always had the best luck. A handsome husband that was a go getter. Two good looking sons that were crazy about her. And she probably had more money than she could spend even though she didn't really work for it.

The liquor was making Brenda bitter. She thought maybe she should probably stop drinking.

Jersey sat up on the couch and turned to her best friend. "What did you just say?"

Brenda not to be punked repeated herself. "I said lucky bitch, and I meant that." She sat up further on the couch, almost challenging her.

"Lucky me? What the fuck is that supposed to mean? Because I don't get it." She felt her temperature rising. She hoped that Brenda got slick so she could finally feel up to doing what she knew she had to.

Brenda scrunched her face so hard that it almost got stuck. "What I mean is everything good is always happenin' to your ass and you don't have to work for it. You got this fine ass husband that make everything happen for you. Then if that's not enough, you got two beautiful sons that would go to hell and back for you. Them niggaz make sure you ain't really gotta lift a finger to live the good life. To me that's because you got some good ass luck."

Jersey took a strong pull off the blunt and blew the smoke in the air. "Sound like you jealous to me, bitch, but you'll get over it. You should've picked your cards better." She continued to bait her, feeling herself heat up.

She was almost where she needed to be.

"Jealous? Bitch, I could've fucked Greed and took this shit away from you a long time ago. That nigga stayed peepin' my every move. Yo lil' skinny ass; what type of hood nigga ain't gon' wanna fuck with a bitch that's thick in all the right places? Every time I walked pass that nigga he was all up in this ass. That's why Slade got to feelin' some type of way about him. He knew that if I wanted to, I could go on that nigga and he would have been balls deep in this pussy. And I would've loved that shit, every inch and every single stroke."

"Fuck did you just say?" Jersey grabbed the lamp off of the table beside them and smashed it across Brenda's head, causing a wide gash to appear on the side of her forehead.

Brenda fell forward and crashed on top of the glass table, shattering it.

Huffing with real anger, Jersey snatched her up by her hair and smashed the marble ashtray into her forehead, further opening the wound that bled profusely.

Brenda groaned. The pain was unbearable and the attack had caught her off guard. She felt woozy and could feel the hot blood seeping down her face like heated syrup. She felt herself being pulled by her hair and thrown over a shoulder.

Rayjon entered on que and picked her up and threw her over his shoulder as his mother opened the back door to her home so he could take Brenda down to the basement where he already had it prepared.

He laid her all the way in the back on top of the black bags that had a hole cut in the middle of them. They were placed on top of the big drain that was usually used by the washing machine to drain itself.

As soon as he laid her down, Jersey straddled her with brass knuckles. She punched her right in the huge gash. "Bitch, don't you ever say nothin' about my muthafuckin' husband! He'd never fuck wit you over me!" She punched her so hard that her wrist went numb for a brief second. Then she picked her up by her head and slammed it backward into the concrete below.

Whoom!

Brenda felt her head crash into the hard surface.

She could barely understand what was going on. Everything was spinning. There was pain coming from everywhere and she could barely breathe. She tried to scream for help, but no sound came out, instead there was a tightening around her neck.

Jersey squeezed her hands together and tried to pop Brenda's head off of her shoulders.

How dare she say some shit like that, she thought.

She tried to remember ever catching her husband looking at her in the way that she spoke of and she absolutely could not.

She slammed her head backward again, this time blood splashed from under it.

Rayjon stood back and watched his mother in action. He couldn't believe how much of a goon she was. She honestly amazed him. He tossed her the big hunting knife and took a step back.

Jersey caught the knife and looked into the bloody face of her friend. She felt a little remorseful. After all, they had been through a lot together.

For a brief second, she had second thoughts on killing her. She felt she had done enough.

Maybe she could bash her head into the concrete some more then she would end up brain dead. She really didn't want to take her life.

Rayjon saw his mother second guessing herself. His father had warned him that *that* could possibly happen.

"Momma, that broad making it seem like she better than you. She talkin' like she could have broken up our family. Every time that Pops was around her, she was secretly choosin' and that mean that if he had wanted to screw her, she would have went. The whole time she was in your face she was plottin' on the head of our family. That chick deserve to die."

Jersey took a deep breath and imagined Brenda and Greed tangled in the sheets with her taking his big pipe from the back. Then she imagined what their conversation would be like afterwards and that did it.

She raised the big knife over her head and brought it down with all of her might just like her husband had shown her, making sure to keep her elbows bent out ward.

The blade sunk into Brenda's face and sliced its way deep into her sinus, getting caught in her throat. She felt like she was swallowing fire. She felt the blade ripping back out of her only to return again, this time it went further into her sinus and hit a part of her brain that stopped her from thinking clearly. Before she could come to terms with her fate, everything faded to black.

Jersey slammed the knife into her face again and again. She could feel her blood popping up and saturating her neck, but she paid it no mind. She continued to visualize the scene of them and it caused her to blank out, stabbing blindly.

Rayjon pulled his mother off of the over killed dead woman.

She at first felt like she was ready to attack him, but he held her firmly.

"It's okay, Momma. She dead now. Ain't nobody gon' take Daddy away from you. Ain't nobody gon' break up this family or knock you off your throne. We seal everything in blood."

Chapter 8

"An all-white Bentley with the gold grill? Aw, hell nall, nigga, now you doin' way too much," Averie said, walking around the Bentley with her mouth wide open. She already knew she was finna have some crazy competition now that her man was rolling a Bentley around California.

Ajani stepped out of the driver's seat and adjusted the red face Rollie before doing the same to his iced gold bracelet.

What the fuck was the use of laying niggaz down if I couldn't reap the benefits of flexing a lil' bit, he thought.

"Ma, you trippin'. This what a Boss supposed to rock when he out here in these streets the way I am." He opened the passenger's door for her and waited until she stepped in, after handing him their son. He placed him into the backseat and strapped him into his booster seat. "Yo, you good, lil' homie?"

Jahni nodded and turned on his tablet. He wanted to see what was popping on YouTube.

Ajani got back into the new whip and stormed away from the curb. The lick with Lando had got them 200 thousand dollars, he already had Rayjon's stash put to the side and with his cut, he was able to finally lease the whip that he always dreamed about. It wasn't nothing like having a Bentley to him. The car screamed he had his game all the way up.

Averie looked like she was sick. She couldn't help but to feel some type of way. Where most females would have been happy that they were rolling in the passenger's seat of a Bentley that their baby daddy drove, she felt the complete opposite because she knew what cars like that attracted. Bitchez, bitchez, and more bitchez. More than likely, most that she couldn't even begin to compete with.

"What's wrong wit you?" he asked, adjusting the steering wheel and flipping the switch so that their seats got cool.

"I don't like this car, baby. I think you should have kept your old one," she said, crossing her arms in front of her.

He shook his head. "You ain't never happy. No matter what I produce, yo lil' ass ain't never happy. Now ain't none of them bitchez that you call yo girlz rolling a Bent. You should feel like you flexin' on them hoez because yo baby daddy winning and theirs ain't."

"Ajani, I keep telling you I don't care about how much money you got long as you keep us with the bare necessities, that's all I ask. You coming' home and laying in the bed with me at night is worth more than a Bentley, any day."

As much as he didn't like what she was saying, he had to respect her for it because she was coming at him like a keeper.

"Women that didn't get caught up on the hype of the game was always the ones you were supposed to wife," his father would say. *"The reason you wife them is because they are wired different. They are programmed to be in the house and taking care of home. All they see is you and your arms wrapped around them is like a bag of money."*

"Baby, don't get shit twisted. I just always wanted to rock something slick like this. Don't think me riding clean gon' cause me to kick you to the curb or lose sight of what we got. I'm more of a man than that. You understand me?" he asked, reaching over and rubbing her chin.

She smiled and nodded her head. "Okay, Daddy, but please just don't let it drive a wedge between us. I honor what we got and you already know how insecure I am."

"I got you."

***

Averie turned around in the full-length mirror and looked at how the dress accentuated her ass. That was one of the reasons she fucked wit Prada, it was like the designer made all of the material strictly for her body type.

Ajani walked up behind her and kissed her neck. "I'm loving how you lookin' in this right now. You always look so much better when you got that high fashion draped across my ass." He smacked it and watched it ripple before pulling out a knot of money so big it was like he had balled up a mini dictionary. All hundreds and fifties.

Averie saw the knot and her eyes got as big as paper plates. "I don't even wanna know where you got all that money from. All I need to know is if we are safe?" She exhaled loudly and felt her stomach do a back flip.

She knew her man was crazy and down for the cause. He was a good provider, too, but he had never worked a 9 to 5 a day in his life. His hustle was the streets. He lived by the steel and though sometimes it excited her, most times it caused her to worry almost to the point of needing to seek psychiatric help.

Ajani was her world. She couldn't imagine life without him. Every time he stepped into those streets, she could barely think about anybody or anything else.

Ajani laughed. "We ain't never safe, ma. It's the life we live. You know how I get down out there. So, we gotta enjoy shit while we got it. I already know I'ma die young, that's why I'm trying to enjoy this shit now."

He felt he already knew what was gon' take place with his life. He had already bagged so many niggaz that he honestly felt like it was bound to happen to him sooner or later.

Averie blinked tears. She felt like she wanted to pass out at just imagining him dying. She swallowed and suddenly the linen draped across her body didn't feel so good. She just wanted to go home and lie in the bed with him. Her chest felt like an elephant was sitting on it.

"Baby, can we just go home and freak all day? "

Ajani adjusted his son on his hip. "Nall ma, I'm 'bout to take lil' man on a shopping spree and get him some new gadgets. Then we gon' drop him off at my mother's crib and I'm taking you out on the town. I wanna put some ice in your ears, too. That's after I done taking you shopping of course."

He adjusted their son one more time. "So, snatch up you a few more of them Pradas, then we gone hit up Eve St. Laurent and get you right. What your Ferragamo game looking like back at home?"

She didn't even care. All she could think about was the fact that he said he was going to spend the rest of the day with her. That was enough to make her feel rich.

***

Rayjon was on his way to pulling out of the BP gas station when his path was blocked by an all-black van. Then three cars pulled into the gas station and parked alongside of him. He reached under the seat and pulled up his Mach .11 ready to start spitting and hitting everything moving.

Camryn was ready to scream. She saw the car doors opening up in front of them and every man that got out had a gat in his hand. They also had red bandanas draped around their necks and faces.

"Yo, ma, I'm 'bout to wet all these niggaz. You stay down. No matter what, you don't pick yo head up. If it look like they about to kill me, I gotta shoot you in the arm so it look like you bleeding', so just play dead or they gon' kill you for real."

Camryn was ready to pass out. So that meant that no matter what she was taking a bullet. That was enough to make her want to get out the car and start running. She knew she didn't have no fucking business in the inner city of Los Angeles, now she had to take a bullet. She was seconds away from becoming hysterical.

Rayjon cocked the Mach and sent his silent prayers to Jehovah. He wasn't scared to die and definitely wasn't about to be the only one going. He slowly rolled down his window prepared to start dumping, when he saw Game get out of one of the Cherry Benz'. He walked right over to Rayjon's Navigator and held his hands up.

"Say, Blood, you either finna get out that Whip and come holler at me or I'm about to give the order and have over a thousand shots sent in yo direction."

Rayjon could feel his heart beat thumping his chest. He didn't know why the gang leader was rolling down on him, or what he really expected, but every fiber of his being was trying to prepare for the inevitable shoot out. "What's it gon' be, nigga? I ain't got all day?" Game pulled two .44 automatics out of their holsters and aimed them at his truck.

Rayjon took a deep breath and looked over at Camryn. She was literally shaking. He started to feel some type of way for her and wished things had riot happened while she was present.

"Yo, I'll come holler at you if you let my woman drive off in my truck. This shit ain't got nothing to do wit her."

Camryn prayed the men would listen. She didn't want to die gunned down in the streets over nothing. She loved Rayjon with all of her heart but she didn't see why she would have to do it from the grave.

Game waved him off. "Nigga, long as you get out, I don't give a fuck about that bitch! She ain't important. But hurry up though before we be out here warring wit LAPD and you."

"Baby, look, I'm finna go holler at this nigga. Take my truck back to my crib and call Ajani. Just let him know what took place." He jumped out of the truck after putting a .45 in the small of his back and walked over to Game.

Game snatched him up roughly and threw him into the black van.

***

"That's what you supposed to have in your ears because you my woman. Every time I get my weight up like this, my first priority is supposed to be you because you so one hunnit and you gave me him," Ajani said, pointing down to their son.

Averie turned her head from side to side as she looked in the mirror at her pink lemonade diamond earrings that Ajani had just spent a fortune on. Every time she moved they sparkled.

"Baby, are you sure I'm worth all of this, though. Can we afford them?"

He held her micro braids out of her face and kissed her on the cheek. "I got this. Even if we couldn't afford it, you would never know because it ain't your job to know. It's mine." He pulled her into his embrace and kissed her on the back of the neck.

After spending nearly three hours at the mall and spoiling both her and their son. They dropped Jahni off with Jersey and he made her put on her new Dolce' and Gabbana dress with the red bottomed five-inch heels, while he himself put on a matching Dolce' and Gabbana fit, with the red bottomed Jordans.

He wasn't about the whole dress shoes thing. He felt like he was still a street nigga and to him street niggaz wasn't supposed to dress like Presidents.

An hour later, they stepped onto the cruise ship with him holding her hand until she got safely aboard. Then he put his arm around her protectively and kissed her cheek. "Baby, this Yacht gon' do a lil' circle around the Bay. It's gon' be about three hours.

I just wanted to take this time to appreciate you." Averie felt like she was getting) ready to cry. The entire evening, he made her feel so special. Even though her baby daddy was a street nigga, he often did things like this for her.

They may have been few and far in between but whenever he did things for her, he went all out.

Ajani did mind seeing all of the white people they had to pass through in order to get to the dining and dancing section of the boat. He wasn't particular about socializing with those not of his kind.

They were all dressed in expensive suite. Their women looked stuck up and bougie. He could tell that most of the men were white collar. Probably judges and lawyers or something like that, he figured.

As they stepped into the dining and dancing portion of the Yacht, the band was just setting up. They all had on white tuxedos, with red bow ties. The music started shortly thereafter and he escorted her to the floor, pulling her into his embrace. "You my baby. You know that, right?"

She closed her eyes and laid her head on to his shoulder. "Yeah, Daddy, but I love when you tell me that over and over again anyway. So, go on, I'm listenin'."

The music was nice and rhythmic. It had a nice jazz feel to it. It screamed elegance. The atmosphere was that of money.

They could smell the ocean. Sounds of champagne glasses clinging was enough to let them know they weren't in the heart of L.A. but in a safe oasis.

"I know I hit them bricks hard but at the end of the day, I love you Averie. I'd kill a nigga dead over you and our son. Everything I do out here in these streets is to make sure that y'all keep eating well."

Averie felt so good that she didn't want to look too far into things. She simply wanted to enjoy her moment with him. She didn't want to ruin it by telling him that none of that mattered more than him holding her at night. Or the fact that she would have been perfectly fine with him working a 9 to 5, just as long as when he got off of work he came home so she could put some food into his belly, before running his bath water. That the only thing mattered to her was him being in the bed with her every night. No, she didn't want to have that argument with him right then. She just wanted to enjoy the moment. Besides, sometimes she liked to hear him flex.

"I'm gon' take us away from here, ma. We ain't finna be in L.A. forever. I'm gon' take us away from here so we can live good and not have to worry about me having to kill a mafucka damn near every day. I mean, I ain't saying I'm tired of killing these fuck-niggaz but I just want better for you and our son. I can't be in these streets forever." He held her more firmly. "You get what I'm tryin' to say?"

"One hundred percent, baby, and I agree." She stepped on to her tippy toes and kissed his lips, as he rubbed her big ghetto booty. Cuffing it the way it was supposed to be cuffed.

Ever since she'd had their kid, her ass had gotten twice as fat and he loved it.

"I'll tell you what, I'm finna grab one of these bottles of Champagne over there and I'm 'bout to take you out on this deck and fuck you from the back while you over look this water. I want some of that pussy. It's calling me."

"I'm wit it," she cooed.

***

Rayjon felt the Mossberg Pump at the back of his head and curled his lip.

"Yo, Game, tell yo nigga to take this shit away from head. This bitch-nigga think its sweet wit me or something?" He turned around and smacked the gun away. "Fuck what wrong wit you, nigga?"

"Game, I'ma smoke this nigga, Blood." Macho was ready to pull the trigger and knock Rayjon's head off. He had heard about Rayjon and his brother and he felt the hood was safer without the two niggaz running around like psycho Outlaws.

"No, you ain't. Nigga, don't no triggers get pulled until I say so and I ain't told you to do shit, so lay yo ass back until I give you that order." He mugged Macho with so much hatred that the other man lowered his head. "Rayjon, just chill, nigga, until we get where we goin'. We should be there in five minutes."

"What's all this about anyway?"

"Like I said, we'll be there in about five minutes and we'll talk business at that time."

Rayjon was heated. He hoped that Camryn had got in touch with his brother, that way by the time he released him, Ajani would already have everything in order for them to go to war.

There was no way he was about to accept that shit laying down. Niggaz putting guns to his head and tossing him around like he wasn't a street Boss. All of it was unacceptable. Had Camryn not been with him, there would have definitely been a bunch of shells dropped all over the streets. He would have rather died than be treated like a bitch the way they were treating him.

"I can tell you one thing, if you don't tell me what I need to know, I'm knocking that head off. That's on my Blood."

Chapter 9

Rayjon was thrown down into the chair inside of a big stale smelling warehouse. They didn't even bother tying his hands or binding his feet, instead he had four men that surrounded him, all pointing assault rifles at his head.

Game came from the back dragging what looked like a woman by her hair. To the left of him, one of his goons was dragging a man by his leg and behind him, another goon was doing the same. They came and dropped all three dead bodies in front of Rayjon.

Game took a step back and tightened his leather gloves on his hands. "Nigga, you wanna tell me what happened to my people?"

Rayjon looked down on to the dead bodies. The woman had a big hole directly in the center of her forehead. There was dried blood all over her face and neck. It looked like somebody had hit her at pointblank range.

To the right of her, the first male's body seemed to have caught one straight to the temple because there was a big hole there. The whole side of his face had dried blood and brain on it.

The last male's face was completely blown in. It looked like somebody had drove a car into it at full speed. Rayjon shrugged his shoulders. "I don't know what the fuck happened. First of all, who is they?"

Game frowned, and knelt down in front of him. "Nigga, are you fuckin' serious?"

Rayjon had to laugh a little bit to calm his temper. He always hated when somebody asked him if he was serious after he told them that he didn't understand something. It was insulting and it made him feel dumb.

His father used to always say, *"Son, if ever somebody ask you are you serious after you have clearly told them that you don't understand something, you walk away from them and break all forms of communication. Never give them the power to feel as if they are better than you or they're teaching you something. Fuck them, walk away and figure things out on your own."*

Remembering that caused him to curl his upper lip in disgust. "Say, Game, I don't know who these people are. So I'm gon' ask you again, who are they?"

Game didn't like nothing about Rayjon or his punk ass brother. If he had his way, he would have put bullets in the both of their heads a long time ago. If it wasn't for their father, Greed, who had the respect of the streets and Chiefs up top.

Game stood up and pointed down at the female first. "That was my baby mother right there. And them two niggaz was her little brothers. This shit happened last night and we missin' about 300 thousand in cash and twenty birds. Now I know how you and yo brother get down, so I'm gon' ask you who hit my people?"

Rayjon looked him over for a long time before answering. He had so many things going through his mind. First off he didn't like how Game was playing the tough role. Ajani had already proved to the nigga that he wasn't in front of the whole school back in the day. He whooped his ass so bad it nearly started an all-out war with their father, Greed, and Game's father, Di'ano, who ran the Blood Bath Bloodz.

The only reason things didn't go that far was because the Blood Baths starting beefing real tough with the Rolling 30's Cripz. They were killing two Bloodz a day, or at least that's what the Bloodz thought. But in actuality, it had been Greed and his two sons picking apart the gang like they were weak ass deer.

"I couldn't tell that was her and I never knew her brothers but that's fucked up, though. That move ain't have nothing to do with me and my people."

Game looked him over closely. He didn't know whether to believe him or not. He wondered if he had done it, if he would have enough balls to keep shit one hunnit.

"I know me and yo brother don't get a long so it wouldn't be nothing for you niggaz to pull up on my bitch while I was out of town and buss this move. Everybody know that since Greed ain't on the scene no more that you lil' niggaz ain't eating like that. It's only a matter of time before y'all get on that Ski Mask shit like y'all old man was on back in the day. The apple don't fall to far from the tree."

"I ain't gon' go back and forth with you over what me and my family holding. I'm telling you that whoever snuffed yo people, ain't from my bloodline. We know what lines to cross and there's a treaty between y'all and us, which means that all Blood Baths are off limits until my old man say so. We honor him over everythang, always have. So once again, that move ain't have shit to do with us." He jumped up ready to leave.

Game backed up and it seemed like a million people were in the room cocking their guns back. There was so much clicking in the room that it echoed off of the walls in the nearly empty warehouse.

"I think you flirting wit death, nigga."

"The way I see it is that I ain't have shit to do with these murders and neither did my people. So don't tell me you finna start a whole war just because you don't like my little brother. Nigga, I'm tellin' you that if you want shit to go down like that, then have one of these bitch-niggaz pull the trigger, then. Fuck y'all waitin' on?"

Game lowered his head and took a deep breath. He was seconds away from blowing Rayjon's head off. He was getting to the point that he was tired of taking orders from the heads up top anyway. He knew that didn't no mafucka in their right mind have enough balls to rob his baby momma and then stank her. The only niggaz that got down like that and had enough gall to do it was Greed's sons. They were untamed and he hated that because they weren't under any organization. They didn't have to follow rules and guidelines, whereas he had to get the nod from the heads up top before he did the absolute most. They gave him permission to snatch Rayjon up, but he was ordered to not kill him.

However, Game swung his toolie with blazing speed, knocking Rayjon off of his feet. "Bitch ass nigga, sit yo punk ass down!" he ordered.

Rayjon felt the steel smash into his mouth, knocking his head backward on his neck. It felt like somebody had hit him at close range with a baseball bat. He felt his body being lifted into the air and the next thing he knew, he was falling on his side and spitting out teeth. He felt the blood dripping off of his chin. He looked up to Game with angry eyes.

"Nigga, I said sit yo bitch ass down. Now either you do that or I'm bodying you. Point blank! I'm tired of you niggaz living off y'all father's respect anyway. Those Blood Bath bitch- nigga, fuck you and him."

Rayjon shot up from the floor and tackled Game before he could begin to think about the consequences. Wasn't nobody about to disrespect his old man under no circumstances. His loyalty for him was sealed in blood, so if the Bloodz was gon' kill him, then they had to come with it.

They landed on top of the dead bodies with Rayjon on top of him. He cocked back and punched him square in the nose busting it like a big berry.

Game felt the punch, and his eyes started to water. Before he could get used to that feeling, Rayjon punched him again and smashed the back of his head into his dead baby mother's stomach.

"Punk ass nigga. Like I said, if you niggaz gon' kill me, then come on wit it. Ain't nobody gon' disrespect my family. I'll kill one…"

Wham!

Big Hurk punched Rayjon in the back of the head, right in the middle of it. Rayjon fell forward as soon as the whole room went dark.

When he woke up, he was in the middle of an alley, ass naked with a bunch of red rags thrown on top of him.

***

"Please, sir, I beg of you, don't do this to my husband. He is a good man. He provides for our family as best he can. We are immigrants from Kuwait. We have no family here in America. He is all that we have, so I beg of you to not take him away."

Aiden finished hanging the man upside down and secured the chains in place. He had purposely left the duct tape from around the woman's mouth so he could hear her beg for her husband's life. The more a person begged the more it made him want to kill them more sadistically. It was like motivation.

Greed had already given him his orders and they were orders that he would follow to the letter. He didn't ask questions, he just made shit happen. He was trying to gain Greed's favor so he could start his own branch of the Ski Mask Cartel.

After he had the man hung the way he needed him to be, he started the chain saw. It came on with a loud roar and sounded like somebody was getting ready to mow their lawn. He squeezed the trigger to get the blade to go faster.

Sarai was beside herself now. She felt that she knew what was coming and she nearly passed out.

"We have money. Lots and lots of money. You can have it all just please don't kill my husband!" she screamed.

Aiden paid her no mind. He didn't give a fuck about her money or nothing of the likes because he was told to take nothing, to just kill and send a message.

"These are words from Kabir that he wants spread around to all of those that wish to oppose him through snitching." He pressed on the trigger and placed the rotating, slicing chain up to the man's nose and began to saw it off. He could hear him screaming through the duct tape.

As soon as Ahmad heard the roar of the chainsaw he shit on himself. If that wasn't bad enough, hearing the name of Kabir let him know that he was about to die. He had found out about his deal with the Feds.

He felt the blade cutting into his nose and it felt like somebody was pouring acid on it. The pain was so bad that he started crying, and shitting at the same.

"Ahhh!" He screamed at the top of his lungs, but his pleas fell on deaf ears.

Aiden saw the man's nose fall onto the floor and went back in on him. He sliced off a huge chunk of his cheek, while his wife screamed in the back ground. His blood spurt into the air and wet up his shoulder and chest, while it oozed down the man's forehead. He didn't stop sawing until he saw bone.

Ahmad felt like his face was being sent through a garbage disposal. He could hear the saw loudly in his ear and then the pain started. Pain that was so unbearable that he didn't know what to do. He started praying for death, while at the same time chastising his self for being so stupid. He should have known that the angry looking man couldn't have been their

Limo driver. But in a haste to get away from his annoying colleagues, he jumped into it anyway and took his wife along for the journey. Now they were out in the woods somewhere and he was being tortured to death.

Aiden was tired of playing. It was time to end the man's life. He took the saw and revved its engine, cut off the man's left leg, then his right arm.

Afterwards, Aiden stepped back and watched as he dangled from the ceiling, looking at his victim like he was slab of beef.

As soon as Ahmad fell to the floor, he started to shake.

He felt the pain of where his arms and legs used to be and his body started to go into shock.

And if that wasn't enough, Aiden straddled him, took pliers and started to pull his tongue out. It was seriously too much for him to physically tolerate, thus his life simply left his body with no more resistance.

Aiden yanked with all of his might until the tongue came out of the man's mouth. As soon as it did, he walked over and put it on the woman's lap.

"Your husband was a snitch. He had to die. If you choose to go that route, this will become your children's fate first, all five of them and then finally your own. Take this tongue and spread the word. We are watching you." With that being said, he released her and watched as she bowed to the ground in worship of him.

Withholding her tears of her bottled emotions, she spoke fretfully, "I swear, I will not speak of your likeness. The message will be sent."

After dropping the lady back off, Aiden set fire to the limo and drove it over the cliff after jumping out of it.

He got back home and peeled off the mask that made him look darker than he actually was.

***

Greed got up from doing a thousand pushups. He flipped on to his back and started his crunches. It was a must that he stayed in shape and in preparation for all forms of battle. He didn't have plans on being in the prison long because everything was falling into place.

After showering, he got back to his room just in time for Aiden to call him and confirm the first lick having been a success. He told him where to pick up the ten thousand that he was to get for the move, and they hung up.

"Say, you got a conjugal man. Your wife is already waiting in the trailer for you, you got ten minutes to get over there." The big white man said with breath so bad that it smelt like he hadn't brushed his teeth in days.

Greed nodded. "Aiight man, I'll be down in less than five." It took him less time than that, though.

As soon as he got into the trailer, Jersey attacked him like he was prey in the wild.

She jumped on him and wrapped her legs around his waist, sucking all over his neck. "I kilt that bitch just like you said I should, baby. I fucked her up good, too, and I feel just like my husband. Like a savage!" She bit into his neck so hard that blood appeared.

Greed tilted his head back to give her better access. He loved when his Lil Momma got down like that. It let him know that she was just like him, and nothing was better than that.

He walked her over to the big bed and threw her down on it aggressively. Her short skirt rose revealing that she wasn't wearing any panties. He pushed it all the way up until it was around her waist. "Daddy finna eat this good pussy, Momma, tell me what you did while I make you cum." He pushed her knees to her chest and licked the length of her vulva, pausing to slurp it up into his mouth.

Jersey arched her back and opened her legs wide. She felt his two fingers going in and out of her at full speed.

"Ohh! Shit, Daddy! I fucked that bitch up. I bussed her shit first wit a lamp and then with those brass knuckles you bought me. Uhhh—shit! I'm cumming already!"

She screamed as he added a third finger and got to running them in and out of her so fast, sucking on her clitoris like a maniac. He knew that was just how she liked it.

She started to buck into his mouth, her juicy pussy squirting like it always did.

He bit all over her thighs with his teeth, then sucked them hard enough to leave hickeys. It wasn't nothing like the taste of his wife. Every time he tasted her, it got better and better.

"Tell me what else you did to that connivin' bitch." He licked in between her ass crack and then straddled her, already having pulled his dick out. He put the big head to her opening and forced it into her wetness. Her heat engulfed him.

"Uhhh—Daddy! Shit, that feels good." She felt him forcing her knees to her chest. Her pussy bussed wide open as his big dick got to knocking down her walls. She did the best she could to squeeze and trap him, but his battering ram was doing damage.

"Tell me, ma." He needed to hear what she'd done. Needed to hear how much of a beast his woman was because she had not always been that way.

When he had first met her, they were teenagers, she was a good girl. Going to church every single day and afraid to use any type of profanity. Her innocence drove him to her. That and the fact that he had never seen a girl as fine as her.

Her parents were abusive, her mother worse than her father. So it didn't take much effort to pry her away from them.

After she became pregnant with their oldest son, they had kicked her out of the house altogether. Out the house and right into the arms of a savage.

He drove all the way into her and pulled back before driving home again. Her pussy was so wet that she was lying in a puddle.

"After I bussed her shit open. Uhh—shit! After I. Daddy, you killin' me right noooow! You killin' this pussyyy!" she screamed, as he balled her up and started going full speed.

"This my shit. This my pussy right here! You belong to me. I'm Daddy! I been Daddy and I'll kill a mafucka over you any day!" All of his muscles had come out. He looked like the incredible Hulk as he drove into her.

Her eyes rolled into the back of her head. She loved the Dick; yearned for it, and her husband made sure that he beat her shit in on beast mode every single time.

As the waves of orgasm shot through her, she felt him biting into her neck and then he picked her up and flipped her on to her stomach, pulling her up to all fours, while he held her small waist and pounded the pussy like a monster. "Tell me, baby!"

"I stabbed that bitch again and again. All in her face, Daddy! I felt her muscles and tissues getting stuck in the knife and I loved that shit. I thought about you and how you raised me to get down." She could feel him deep in her stomach.

Greed smacked her ass and watched it ripple while his dick drove into her harder and faster until finally he was dumping his seed into her belly. "Uh—uh! Shit, Momma. That's my baby right there."

Chapter 10

Ajani picked up his phone and looked at the screen. It said he had fifty missed calls. He scrunched his face and got a little irritated.

What Rayjon doing calling me fifty times? That nigga must have lost his damn mind.

Averie came up behind him and kissed him on the cheek. "What's the matter, baby? Why you lookin' at your phone like that?" She prayed nothing bad had happened.

"Really I'm tripping because my brother called me fifty times and now that I'm trying to hit him up he ain't responding. That don't seem strange to you?"

She shrugged her shoulders. "He probably fucking something. You already know how y'all get down. Check on Facebook and see if he put up any new statuses or if he on there."

As soon as he was about to do that he heard a loud beating on their front door. The beats were so loud it woke up their son. He started screaming at the top of his lungs.

Ajani pushed Averie toward the back room and grabbed the Mach .11 from under the couch. Cocking it back, he crouched down and slowly crept to the window to peer out of it. Before he could pull the curtain back, the beating started again.

He felt chills go down his spine. "Man, who the fuck is it?" Ajani had visions of someone bussing through the door. But he knew from past experience that his bullets could still kill whoever was on the other side.

Rayjon felt ready to snap. "Nigga, this yo muthafuckin' brother! Open this punk ass door, I'm naked!"

Naked?

Ajani damn near broke his neck trying to get the door opened up. As soon as it opened, Rayjon stormed in, rubbing his shoulders. He had a sheet wrapped around him.

"What the fuck happened? Who did this shit?" Ajani eyed his brother curiously.

"Them bitch ass Blood niggaz. They knocked out my fuckin' teeth and more." He pointed to his grill and dropped the sheet, so he could see all of the bruising.

Ajani's eyes got as big as saucers. "Them bitch ass niggaz did that?" Tears started to come down his eyes almost immediately, as he looked up at his big brother. It had always been that way ever since they were little kids. Whenever one of them got hurt and the other was present it was like he was in the same amount of pain. Ajani felt the tears rolling down his cheeks and then his lip slowly curled into a snarl. "On everything I love, I'm finna murder everything! Ain't no way in hell we finna accept this!"

Rayjon ran his tongue across the spaces where his two front teeth used to be. "That fuck nigga, Game, think we snuffed his baby momma and her brothers. He got hit for a few hundred thousand bands and a gang of birds."

"That ain't have shit to do wit us. I mean, I wish we would've hit that lick, but we didn't. Did we?" Ajani asked him just to make sure.

He shook his head. "Hell nall. Pops said that them niggaz was off limits. That's the only reason I ain't been killing them on sight. But after this shit, we gon' have to re-evaluate some things. I'm 'bout to call his phone right now. Momma took him the new one, right?"

Ajani nodded. "Yeah, today was their conjugal visit, that's when they usually switch phones. But I ain't got the new number, yet, so we gotta wait anyway."

Rayjon flopped down on the couch still running his tongue across his gums. "I need some of that girly. Go bring me at least an ounce of powder. I gotta numb this pain I'm going through right now." He laid his head back on the couch with his eyes closed.

Ajani felt like he wanted to kill everything red. His brother had been hurt and he wasn't there to help him. He felt less than a man. He felt like he had let his brother down.

He got to imagining the Bloodz killing him and throwing his body into the ocean and that made him sick. He promised to his self that he was going to kill Game. He was going to kill him in cold blood and love every minute of it.

***

Aiden waited until the Arab woman came out of the office building and stood on the curb obviously waiting for a cab. It was just his luck that the last two had picked up their occupants and drove off just before the woman stepped outside.

He slowly pulled in front of her and smiled. It had only been twenty minutes prior that he'd sat in the back of the same cab that he was currently driving.

He ordered the man to drive into the alley and after he followed his directives, he dumped him into the big metal garbage can and blew his brains out the front of his face.

It took him all of five minutes and he felt nothing.

Khadijah felt like her prayers had been answered when Aiden's cab rolled up in front of her. She was praying that she wouldn't have to get into one of those crowded Ubers that seemed to be patrolling around.

She opened the back door and climbed in. It smelled like Frankincense and baby powder inside.

"Can you take me to Lake and Western? I have a very important business meeting that I need to get to in thirty minutes.

If you get me there in twenty, there is a big tip in it for you." She smiled and waited for his reaction.

She didn't mind Jamaicans, most of them were extremely talkative, which was okay by her, but this one seemed to be the opposite. He didn't even say a word.

"I'm sorry. Did you hear me?"

Aiden stepped on the gas after nodding his head at her. He locked both doors in the back and got onto the highway.

He flipped the fake dread locks over his shoulder and looked in the rearview mirror. "Kabir wants to know how you could betray him and take your husband's side over his, when you're his sister?"

Kahdijah's heart started to pound so hard it was making her chest hurt. "It's okay, sir. Can you please let me out at the next exit?"

Boo-Wa!

The gun spit and the bullet slammed into her shoulder, knocking meat out of her back. Before she could come to the terms of being shot she had pissed on herself.

Ahhhhh! What have you done?" she screamed and grabbed her shoulder in pain.

"Answer my question, lady," Aiden said, lazily. He had been up for three days without sleep. Tooting so much cocaine that his mind wouldn't stop racing. He had a list to fulfill and he was going to fulfill it before he would be able to lay down for a good night's rest.

Kahdijah held her shoulder as the blood seeped through her fingers. "What the fuck is the question?"

"If I have to repeat myself, I'm going to shoot you again."

She started to panic. She didn't want to feel that hot lead. Her shoulder felt like somebody was trying to pull it off of the bone. "You tell Kabir that I didn't take any sides. I was thinking about my children. If I had backed him, I would have lost them and their father and he wasn't worth the risk."

Aiden took the cell phone and handed it back to her. "Here. Why don't you tell him that? Better yet." He snatched it back from her and hooked up the phone so it could go through the speakers in the car. "Speak, lady."

"Hello?" she whimpered.

"Yes, is this my sister sounding like she is in distress? Oh boy, I wonder where Sadiq is now when you need him?"

Khadijah broke into a fit of tears. "Don't do this to me, Kabir. We are family. You have to remember that." The stinging got worse in her shoulder.

"Remember that? Hey, my friend. Do me a favor and shoot her in the other shoulder."

Boo-Wa!

The bullet knocked a hole into her other shoulder, sending her flying backward. The pain was so intense that she passed out.

Aiden leaned into the back and smacked the shit out of her, jolting her awake. "Say, bitch, wake yo as up. I can't take pride in that pain you going through if you back there sleep and shit," Aiden hollered.

Kahdijah opened her eyes and it felt like the pain got ten times worse. She didn't know why God was allowing her to go through such tribulations. Maybe it was because she had been stealing from the Mosque and taking kickbacks. Or the fact that she had taken more than ten percent of the money raised that was supposed to help out the refugees back in her country.

Either way, she felt like the punishment was ten times worse than the crimes she'd committed.

"Khadijah, wake up and face this like a woman! Why would you go against me? Your own brother for a man that is nothing more than a rotten pedophile?"

She shook her head from right to left. Blood pouring out of her wounds. She started to feel dizzy and like she wanted to pass out. "I can't do this right now. I'm bleeding."

"Answer me, you filthy whore! I've always stood by you and this is how you treat me? You help the Americans to lock me up and threaten to throw away the key! How dare you?"

Aiden turned on to the exit ramp. After rolling for about a hundred yards, he came to the light and made a left headed for the woods on the outskirts of town. He felt his stomach growl and paid it no attention.

"The Quran says that I am supposed to honor and respect my husband first and foremost. Nothing is to come before him. Why can't you get that through your head? I never turned my back on you. I was just walking beside him first."

"Well as soon as Sadiq is found, I'm going to show him what it means for someone to stand by him. I'm also getting rid of all of your sons. I can't risk them turning into the likes of you and him. Rest in Jinnat, my sister. Finish her."

By this time, Aiden had pulled along the dirt path. He stopped the cab and threw it in park. Getting out of the car, he opened the back door and pulled her out by her hair, dropping her to the ground.

Khadijah was in no position to fight. Her arms felt like there were two Semi's parked on top of them. The blood loss had her woozy. She felt the man dragging her by her hair and she couldn't even put up a fight. She started to recite the Afatihah in her mind and begged Allah for forgiveness.

Aiden dragged her all the way to the grave that had been dug in her honor. He yanked her up by the neck and put the gun to her forehead, making sure that she was positioned correctly.

Boo-Wa! Boo-Wa! Boo-Wa!

Khadijah saw the bright lights and then it felt like somebody had kneed her in the forehead with all of their might. She tried to reason with what was happening but then she felt the back of her head open up and the whole world faded to red and then black.

Aiden dropped her in the grave and wiped his face. Her blood felt hot and there was little pieces of brain all over the ground. They looked like little shrimp. He picked one up and squished it in his fingers before flicking it into the grave along with her body.

He walked back to the small cabin, mumbling to himself, not really saying anything at all. It was just the way his brain worked at times.

***

Greed put up his shit blanket and ducked down, looking into his phone at Rayjon's gums. "You mean to tell me that them punk ass Bloodz did that?" He clenched his jaw in obvious anger.

Just telling his father what had taken place had Rayjon ready to kill something. He knew that his old man was crazy about him. He would always tell him that. He was his first born son and he would always tell him stories about all that he and his mother had to go through while she was pregnant with him.

Even after his birth things weren't so easy. He wasn't even three years old before his tonsils had to be taken out. A surgery that almost made his father kill the doctor because he thought he was hurting him.

"Yeah, Pops, them niggaz talking about our family bodied his baby moms and her brothers. We ain't have nothing to do with that, though."

"I bet you the next ones won't be able to say that. I ain't honoring this crap. I refuse to." Ajani turned the bottle of Patron up. He was ready to do some damage. He was praying that his old man would give them the nod.

He knew where Game's mother stayed and he wanted to knock her shit off. He didn't give a fuck if she had something to do with it or not.

Greed lowered his head. He couldn't even look into his son's face because it was killing his soul. Their whole life he had made it a point of never allowing them to be hurt under his guidance. Now he didn't know what to do. He knew he had to act out of smarts and not anger, though. That was always easier said than done.

Rayjon was his heart. His first born.

"Pops, what you gon' let us do, man? We need to know this right away," Rayjon said, eyeing the Mach .11 from across the room.

He had the extended clip that went along with it. It spit 150 bullets total and every time he barely tapped the trigger, it released three bullets rapidly. It even had a green beam on top of it. He wanted to put that bad boy to use. He needed to.

Greed rubbed his temples. "Look, for now y'all fall back and collect yourselves. I gotta take care of some business at the top of the pyramid. After that concludes, then I'll give the order. Until then, nobody moves. Do y'all understand me?"

Ajani didn't know if he heard him correctly. He had to lean down and stick his face into the phone. "You saying we finna let this ride over night? We finna just roll over and tarnish our family name? What we finna switch our shit from Edwards to what? I feel…"

Jersey came into the room and smacked him so hard that the bottle fell out of his hand and rolled under the couch with liquor spilling out of it. "I told you to watch yo mouth when you in front of me or your father. Now if you can't handle that liquor, then you pour that stuff out!" she demanded, giving him the look of death.

Ajani's mouth was stinging so badly that he wanted to shoot up the ceiling. He was pissed and what made it even worse was that he knew he was in the wrong. He didn't have no business cursing in front of his mother or father and he knew it.

He looked up to her from one knee. "I'm sorry, Momma. I know better than that. I ain't mean no disrespect to you or my old man." He turned toward the phone. "You hear me Pops?"

Greed nodded, "Look, I'll be in touch. Nobody move until I say so."

As soon as he hung up the phone with his family, he removed the brick from the wall in his cell and slid the phone inside of it. Placing the brick back and throwing a shirt over his beater, he opened his door and stepped onto the gallery.

Lox saw him and came over after securing his shank on his hip. He nodded to Killa and he did the same. They looked Greed up and down and could tell that something wasn't right. He looked like he was ready to kill something.

"Look, I might have to kill Suge if he don't tell me what I need to hear in regards to my boys. Some bullshit just happened to my oldest kid and I ain't honoring just no any explanation. If we gotta go tonight, then that's how it's gon' go."

Killa rolled his head around on his neck. "I'm gon' go rally the troops. On some real shit, I hope it go down. I'm ready to body them red niggaz. If we can hit some of them blue bitchez too, that'll be perfect."

Lox frowned. "Is lil' homie and them straight out there or do I gotta have some of the hood ride down on them?"

"Yeah, he good, but they knocked out his front teeth, which means that my son shed blood. Whenever one of mine shed blood, that mean a hundred of theirs have to, too. "

Lox smacked his hands together and rubbed. "That's that *Cartel Greed* we been looking for. Chief, on everything whenever you ready to make shit happen, we wit you one hundred percent."

Greed ducked back into his room and grabbed his 12 inch shank. He was ready to spill some blood, somebody had to pay a price for his kid, that's just the way it was going down.

While Greed was getting strapped up, a CO's voice came over the loud speaker. "*Rec will be in five minutes. All outside rec will be in minutes!*"

Two minutes later, Greed and his crew waited inside of the big laundry department. In order to get to the building, one would have to make a right and go directly down the corridor that led to the double doors that allowed the inmates to go outside.

Greed had already sent word that he needed to speak with the Chief of the Bloodz. But to further drive home his point, he had Lox and Killa on the watch to make sure his words weren't ignored.

They stood posted by the double doors on the lookout for Suge. The orders were for them to snatch him up if he refused to meet with their Chief, and if things got bloody, then so be it.

Chapter 11

Suge came into the laundry room with twelve men behind him. He was a big fat bright skinned man, with a long scar on the side of his face. He held up one hand as he stepped into the room. "Look, Greed, I ain't got time for this shit today. I hope you ain't trying to take things there."

Greed jumped off of the long table that was used for folding clothes and walked toward the nigga. Every man in the room was on edge. Both Chiefs were hot heads and they expected their souljahs to be relentless and to kill without mercy. If things popped off, it was going to be an ugly scene.

Lox gave the guard that was in charge of that area a thousand dollars. "Yo, we need about an hour. Make sure we straight and whatever happens in this mafucka ain't got nothing to do wit you. We know how to clean up our own mess."

The big, bald, white man, nodded and closed the doors behind him. He went to the front of the corridor and locked it off.

As soon as Lox came back into the room, where everybody else was, he gave Greed the nod.

Greed got in front of Suge and rolled his neck around on his shoulders. "What happened to my son, Suge?"

Suge turned his head slightly to the side and looked Greed up and down as if he really didn't want to talk to him. He didn't like the man and what he represented. He felt like he was an untamed animal with no restraint. He had no structure of the mind. Everything he did seemed to be impulsive.

"One of my safe houses got hit. A lot of bread missing and we took three casualties including my son's baby mother. Word around town is that yo boys been knocking heads off and robbing everything. Then the day after our hit, your youngest son roll up in Cali in a brand new Bentley, with a red faced Rolex. Just putting two and two together."

Greed frowned so hard that his face hurt. "Just putting two and two together and what? Nigga. He started to clench his jaw off and on.

"Well, we felt like your boys had something to do with it. I mean, all of the pieces of the puzzle add up."

Greed tilted his head toward the ceiling and took a deep breath. "Move, nigga!" he said, taking a step back from Suge.

Suge looked him up and down but took heed to his advice, just in time because Greed reached back and connected with Suge's first line of security's jaw.

Bam!

He hit him so hard that he flew backward.

The whole room was on edge but Greed didn't give a fuck. As the big 6'6", 320-pound, baldheaded, black man stumbled backward, he rushed him and punched him again straight in the chin. Before he could hit the pavement, Greed scooped him into the air and dumped him on his head, busting that shit wide the fuck open.

Blood formed in a pool around his face, but he wasn't done with his ass. He flipped him over and punched him again and again in the mouth. Harder and harder. Knocking out tooth after tooth. He even turned his head to the side so his face lied on the concrete.

As soon as he figured he had knocked out enough teeth, he gathered them into his hand, went and dropped them at Suge's feet. "Mafuckas better tell me something better than what you assumin', because I ain't goin'. I'm not geein' for that."

All of the Bloodz behind Suge was ready to kill something. They didn't like the way shit was looking because in that moment, it looked like Greed was flexing on their Mob.

Peeto felt the blade taped to the small of his back and he prayed he would get to use it.

"Check this out, Blood. I ain't give no order for your boy to be touched. My son took that upon himself and he's going to be disciplined accordingly. What you just did to my General is enough to start a war in here, and out there. But by me knowing who you are and where your connections lie, I'm forced to give you a G-pass," said Suge.

"I don't need no G-pass! Nigga, I am that G and I tried to keep shit cordial wit yo organization but it seem like y'all don't understand what a treaty mean. Due to that fact, I'm forced to unleash my lil' ones. This shit ain't got nothing to do with me and you. We gon' let our kids settle this shit. Seven days of blood, nigga. Do you trust yo seed to survive? Because I trust mine."

Suge walked into his face and looked him dead in the eyes. "You sure you want shit to go down like that? My hand stretched all the way to New York and back. I got red niggas all over the map. I can't see two lil' niggas fucking our whole mob over like that."

Greed smiled, "I guess you trust yo seed, then."

***

Rayjon looked at his new grill in the mirror, while Ajani stood behind him. It was all gold with white diamonds on each tooth. Every time he opened his mouth, it sparkled brightly. He ran his tongue across them and smiled. "Them bitch niggas ain't do nothing but make me step my game up."

Ajani kissed him on the cheek. "Can't nobody fuck wit us, big bro. These niggas mad because we handsome, we don't ask nobody for shit and we stand tall on the foundation that is our family." He rubbed his tongue across his grill as well, having gotten an identical grill as his brother, in a show of solidarity.

Rayjon turned around and hugged him. "We gon' bring heat to these niggas. I can't wait 'til Pops give that word." He pulled out a bank roll so fat that it looked like a balled up Bible.

He walked to the counter and looked over the pretty brown skinned female with the ear piece in her ear. She seemed to be engaged in a conversation on her phone but when she saw him holding all of that cash, she ended it.

"You ready to pay for your grill work?" she asked with eyes wide open.

Ajani laughed. "Them bankrolls make a mafucka straighten up and act right, don't they?"

She smiled and for the first time, they noted that she had an all gold grill with pink diamonds on every tooth. It fit her to the tee and made her look like a fine ass high priced boss bitch.

Rayjon was fighting within himself to not get at her. Had it been any other day he would have been all over her, trying to see what her world be like but they were awaiting the call from their father to know what their next steps should be.

If he pulled the trigger on an all-out war, there would be no time to be laid up screwing new pussy. Their obligations would be murder and the protections of their family's throne.

Ajani leaned over the counter. "Say, what's yo name, shorty?" He smiled and looked her up and down.

Passion knew what the game was all about. She made it seem like she had to grab something off of the top shelf behind her. When she turned around, she was sure they were going to peep her fat ass booty in her Jordache jeans. The jeans were one and a half sizes too small. So tight that she had to lay on her back on her bed and struggle to get them on. As soon as she turned around, both brothers damn near hugged each other. Her ass looked like something outta a Straight Stuntin' magazine.

She was so thick that it looked like if she made the wrong move, she was gon' bust out of those jeans.

"Aye! Shorty, look I'm trying see what all that be like. I'll take you out tonight. Wherever you wanna go," Ajani said, without looking up. His dick was already starting to rock up.

All Rayjon could do was laugh. "Let me pay for my work then y'all can holler."

Passion looked both brothers over and nodded her approval. "I really ain't got no free time like that, homeboy. But you can come down to my club tonight and see me dance. I'll try my best to set aside some time for a casual conversation if that's cool," she said to Ajani, as Rayjon paid for both he and his brother's teeth work.

***

Aiden walked around the cabin brushing his teeth. It seemed like it was cooler this morning because his toes were freezing. He stepped over the little boy he had tied up under the window sill and closed the window, nearly tripping over the little boy's brother on the other side of him.

Back in the bathroom he spit his toothpaste into the sink and gargled mouthwash. He hated tasting a stale breath. It made him feel like a bum.

He grabbed his face towel and ran hot water over it, pouring a little rubbing alcohol into it before running it all over his face. After he finished that, he applied his eczema cream.

Five minutes later, he was hoisting the first little boy onto the metal table and holding him steady while he wiggled and screamed into the duct tape around his mouth.

Brandon screamed at the top of his lungs. He screamed louder and louder, praying that somebody could hear him. He didn't know why the man had snatched him from his bed in the middle of the night. He didn't know why he and his siblings had been bound and gagged.

The yellow faced man looked like he was crazy. He feared for his life, so he hollered and hollered but to no avail.

Aiden took the hammer and swung it downward with all of his might, connecting with the little boy's forehead. It put a big hole directly in the center. He raised it and slammed it down again. This time directly into his cheek. His little legs stopped moving almost immediately.

When Brandon saw the man raise the hammer over his head, he got so scared. Then he brought it down and he felt it slam into his forehead. It felt like his skull was being kicked in and then the pain shot from his face all the up to his brain and down his spine. It hurt so bad that he wanted to run.

Before he could get used to that blow, the second one came. He felt hot liquid running down his face and then he went to sleep.

Aiden hacked off his arms and legs, and dropped them into the big container. He walked over and hoisted the boy's brother onto the bloody metal table, not wasting no time. He raised the hammer and smashed it into the boy's forehead just like he had done his older brother. One strong smash and the little boy stopped kicking immediately with his blood and bones popping up from the table.

Aiden brought the hammer down again before slightly turning the boy on his side, aiming to hit his temple. He knew that if he connected with it, it would kill him for sure, and that's what he was going for.

Bam! He brought the hammer down so fast and hard that it got stuck into the side of his head. He wiggled it, in order to get it back out.

The first blow caught Brayden off guard. Soon as it hit his little skull, it bashed it in and put a hole in his brain. The second blow that struck his temple was pointless. He was already dead.

Aiden hacked off of his arms and legs, just as he had done his sibling's. After he finished, he dumped them in the big container along with his torso.

Next, he walked over and snatched up the teenaged girl by her hair and drag her across the floor. He picked her up and flung her on the table, with her struggling against him. As soon as he got her to where he needed her to be, he snatched the tape off of her mouth.

"Arrrgh! Arrrgh! Please don't do this! Don't do this to me." Brandy screamed. "Help me! Help me!"

Aiden smiled, he turned his head to the side. "Little momma, why are' you making all of that noise? Do you think it's helping your case at all?"

Brandy was shaking horribly. She was shaking like it was freezing cold in the room and she was naked. "Puhleeze, mister, puhleeze don't do this to me. I'm only a kid. I'm too young to die." Tears ran down her cheeks. She looked so vulnerable.

Aiden leaned down and kissed her on the forehead. "So how old do you think you need to be before you're eligible to die?"

Her eyes got as big as paper plates. "What?"

"You said that you're too young to die. So tell me how old should you be before the bucket is kicked from under you. I just want to know."

Now she knew she was dealing with a lunatic. She didn't answer his questions. She noticed the huge blue, bloody container, and it freaked her out. "I don't know. But definitely not at sixteen. That's way too young."

Aiden grabbed her by the hair roughly. "My babysitter killed my sister when she was only nine. I was beaten so savagely by my father when I was four years old that I died twice before as they tried bringing me back. I was eleven when I got shot three times. I died then, too, but once again they brought me back. I've watched more than enough kids die. It's normal. Everybody has a clock that eventually goes out. You can't stop it. It's preset before you're born. When the alarm sounds, you deal with it. There is no other way."

"But I..." She broke into a fit of tears. "I just don't want to die. I'm supposed to go to prom this year and it'll be my first time going. I already have my dress picked out and my mother was going to do my hair. I wanted to..."

Aiden swung the hammer and slammed it directly into her face. It got stuck immediately. He snatched it out and swung it again implanting it into her temple. Then yanked it out again and brought it down onto her forehead. He went crazy swinging and swinging. Knocking big chunks of meat out of her face. He turned the hammer around to use the nail extractor part and went back to work. The goal was to fulfill the list that Greed had given him.

***

As soon as Ajani walked into the house, Stacey rushed him, jumped into his arms and wrapped her legs around his body.

"It's my birthday, Ajani! It's my birthday! You promised to take me out. I want to spend the whole day with you!"

Rayjon started laughing. He knew the little girl had a thing for his brother. He had told him on numerous occasions how hard it was for him to not smash her. He was trying to wait until her eighteenth birthday. And here it was. All he could do is shake his head.

Ajani felt her kiss his cheek. He looked over his shoulder and saw Averie glaring at him with the look of pure evil. Her demeanor said she was ready to snap. She gave him the *come here* signal with her finger and walked toward their bedroom.

Rayjon peeped the whole scene. "Look like you got a lil' dilemma on your hands, bro." He snickered and ran his tongue across his new grill.

He put Stacey down and she looked up to him like she was disappointed. "This isn't fair. I've been so cool for two weeks straight. I tried to let you guys spend as much time as possible alone so that when my birthday rolled around I could spend some time with you." She stomped her foot. "And today is supposed to be my day."

Ajani rubbed her chin. "Chill out, ma, let me go in here and holler at her and see what's good. After I come back, me and you 'bout to bounce and spend some time together. I did make you that promise and I'ma man of my word."

As soon as Ajani got into the big bedroom, Averie was standing by the dresser lotioning her hands. He closed the door behind him. and turned up the radio because he figured they were about to do some yelling. Luckily, their son was at Pre-K.

"Averie, what's the problem?"

She scrunched her face and tilted her head toward the ceiling. She exhaled and looked him straight in the eye in obvious irritation. "You finna fuck that lil' bitch today, ain't you?"

She already knew what the answer was but she just wanted to see if he was going to keep it real and uncut. She had watched Stacey strategically pick out her outfit. She took a very long shower and did her hair all up. She even peeped her slipping into the Victoria Secret's Pink collection lingerie, so she knew the little girl was preparing herself for her baby daddy and it pissed her off. She had visions of killing her or at the very least, whooping her ass until she decided to pursue somebody else.

"Yeah, I'm definitely about to smash her lil' ass. She 18 now, so it's good," he said, rubbing his chin. He didn't really want to hurt his baby mother, but he refused to lie to her.

The fact of the matter was that he had plans on fucking the shit out of Stacey. He had to be the first nigga to hit that pussy. He felt like he was doing everybody a favor by waiting until she turned 18 because in California the age of consent was 17.

So yeah, he kept shit real with her and hoped that it didn't break her heart.

Averie felt like she had been gut punched. As much as she appreciated the truth, it was still painful to hear that reality. She tried to fight the tears from falling from her eyes, but it was so hard. "Why, Ajani?" She looked at him and blinked tears.

He felt his stomach drop. He hated hurting her, but he just had to have some of that young pussy. He and Stacey had been flirting around ever since she was 16. Her body was so cold that it was hard to not lust after her. He had never seen an ass so big on such a little frame. He had to hit that shit.

"Averie, I been wanting to fuck her since day one. You see how she walk around with them panties all in her booty and shit. What nigga wouldn't wanna hit that? And it ain't got nothing to do with me not respecting you, because I do. I just love pussy. I'm gon' always make sure the home front straight, though."

"So it's okay if I love dick so much that I go out and fuck who I wanna fuck?"

He frowned, "If you want me to whoop yo muthafuckin' ass and kill that nigga, then be my guest." He always choked her ass up even speaking on some shit like that.

What type of nigga would let his baby momma go out and fuck just any random nigga?

He felt it would be cool if they weren't living together and trying to raise their son in one house. But since they were, that shit was just unacceptable.

"See, that's what the fuck I mean right there. So then why do you get to do it?" She felt like she wanted to cry again.

She hated when he pretty much bullied her into getting his way. She felt she didn't have any legs to stand on because if she tried to do the shit that he did, he would wind up killing the nigga and kicking her ass. Then after that, only God knows what he'd do. But she was sure he'd kick her out into the street.

"I ain't fuckin' no random bitch, she basically live here and she yo lil' cousin. We know where she been and how she get down. You fuckin' wit one of them nasty ass niggas out there like that we don't know what the fuck they got."

She shook her head. "So it's cool for you to fuck my family, then?" She couldn't believe they were having this conversation.

He bugged his eyes out. "Yeah, that's Stacey. I gotta hit that shit."

"Awright then, if you fuck Stacey today, then let me fuck Rayjon."

Chapter 12

"Father in the name of Jesus, I come to you humbly and sub-missive as one flesh with my husband, asking for forgiveness for our entire family. Please continue to walk with us and pro-tect us from harm. Wash our hands as white as snow though they may be currently saturated in blood. In Jesus Holy and Precious name I pray. Amen."

Jersey reached over and rubbed Aiden's back, then they both got up and left out of the church with her behind the wheel of the 2018 Mercedes Benz truck. "How are you doing, nephew? I haven't seen you around in a few weeks."

Aiden put his seat belt across his chest and made himself comfortable. If there was one person that he loved in the world, it was his Aunty Jersey. Out of everybody, she just seemed to get him.

"I'm good, Aunty. I been trying to get a hold of myself but it's just hard." He felt the sleep trying to take over him. He bucked open his eyes and took a deep breath before blowing it back out.

"Is it the killing that's getting to you?" She started the truck and drove off on her way to Thylon's Rib Shack. They had the best ribs in the whole state of California and she made it her business to always eat there after her Friday prayers that she sent to Jehovah from Kingdom Hall.

Aiden shook his head. "Nall, I love taking lives. I feel like that's what I was put on this earth for. I feel like God put me here to take people out." He scrunched his face and started talking with his hands. He made the choking motion. "When I'm killing somebody, it's the only time I feel I have a pur-pose. It makes me feel alive and powerful. It's all I think about," he said, going into his shirt pocket and pulling out the fat blunt.

"Can I spark this?"

Jersey really was not in the mood to smoke after cleansing herself, but decided that it would be okay if he smoked. "Go ahead, baby."

He let his seat back a little bit and put the flame to the blunt's tip. As soon as the fire hit it, Jersey could tell that the blunt had been mixed with crack. It smelled like weed and burnt sugar.

Aiden took the smoke and inhaled it harshly. Before he could blow it out, Jersey let down his window.

"Baby, I really don't like that Primo smell in my truck, so blow that out your window for me and let's finish our talk. Do you think you like killing so much because of what your father did to you and your brother?"

Aiden felt himself start to shake as he thought back on the abuse. His father had a habit of getting drunk and beating him and his brother into comas. He was just as bad with their mother, too, until Aiden and his brother, August, killed him while he slept.

One day, their mother came home and found the boys trying to burn his body in the basement. They had told her they were trying to get rid of him before she got home because they didn't want to get a whooping.

He turned to Jersey and nodded, then broke into tears. "I don't know why my father hated me and my brother so much. I don't know why he tried to kill us on so many occasions. But every time I kill somebody, it's him that I'm seeing. I think that's why I love it so much. August get back in town this afternoon, and I don't know how we're going to handle being back in town with each other. He said he left forty bodies back in Madison. He can't conquer the urges either."

Jersey pulled into parking lot, leaned over and put her arm around him. "It's okay. You're a beast, nephew," she said. "I love you, and so do my husband and our boys."

"Even though I live to kill?"

Jersey shrugged her shoulders. "Hey, it does feel good to kill something every now and then. Even I gotta admit that. So don't think that you're alone. When you get your urges just be smart. Kill but kill in a way that both satisfies and is going to allow you to live to see many more days in freedom and whenever you need an ear, I'm here. Okay?"

He nodded and kissed her on the cheek. "Thank you. I needed to hear that."

"No problem, now let's go eat, it's my treat."

***

Ajani pushed Stacey onto her stomach across the bed and pulled up her red laced panties by the leg holes so that the material got stuck in her ass. Both brown globes were exposed, jiggling. He leaned down and bit into her right cheek.

"Umm, baby, I been waiting for this. I been so patient," she moaned and arched her back.

Her stomach felt like it had a million butterflies in it. Every time he touched her, it seemed as if he was emitting electricity onto her skin.

He spread her legs further and rubbed her pussy through the material, trying to see if he could get her to leak through it. It didn't take long before he was able to rub his fingers together and they were sticky.

A huge puddle formed right over where her hole was. He kissed it, licking the cloth. Sniffing her young sex lips that protruded through the material.

Finally, after becoming too excited, he pulled the panties to the side and exposed her sex lips. They were fat and swollen. Dripping a clear gelatinous fluid, he licked directly between her lips and tasted her pearl tongue.

"Ummm-hmm, baby, that feels so good. Please eat my lil' pussy up." She spread her legs wider, bussing it open for him. She put her hand under herself and spread her lips apart.

Ajani sucked up her pussy like a vacuum cleaner, sending his tongue up and down her crease, loving the way she tasted. She had a fresh scent wafting from her hole that was driving him crazy.

***

Averie took Rayjon's dick and stroked it up and down, looking him in the eyes. At first, she was afraid to sleep with her baby daddy's brother, but Ajani had told her it was okay. That she was basically keeping it in the family.

After Rayjon said he was down for it, she became okay with the idea. Besides she couldn't deny that she had always found him super attractive. He was slimmer than Ajani, but he had those manly yet girl facial features that made him look so damn fine.

Though she had never thought about crossing that line, now that she was given the green light, she wanted to enjoy it. She pulled the skin back on his dick and sucked the head into her mouth, stroking it at the same time.

Rayjon reached across her back and smacked that big ass ghetto booty that he had always peeped. Quiet as kept, he would have been down for fucking her years ago if his little brother would have gave him permission.

Averie was thick as a muthafucka. He didn't mind the few stretch marks that were on her stomach because he knew they were her stripes for bringing his nephew into the world. His father had always said that a man was supposed to appreciate a woman's stretch marks because they were her war wounds. Just like niggas got them in the field of battle when they were taking a life or trying] to survive a hit on their life. A woman got her war wounds from bringing lives into this world.

He smacked her ass and rubbed downward until his fingers were playing in her bald pussy. It leaked like she was peeing. That told him she was ready for the dick. He slid two fingers into her as she sucked up and down his pole.

Averie spread her knees further apart to give him better access. She felt his fingers slip into her and she almost came. She popped his dick out of her mouth.

"Look, Rayjon, I can keep sucking yo dick if you want me to, but I want you to fuck me right now. I need you inside of me. I want all of this pipe, please."

Rayjon backed up and pushed her over the bed. He got behind her and rubbed his fat dick head up and down her crease until her lips opened like a mouth, then he slid into her warmth and pushed it all the way home until her ghetto booty was up against his stomach all soft and juicy.

Averie closed her eyes and started to moan at the top of her lungs. He had stuck his forbidden dick deep within her channel. "Aww shit! Rayjon, fuck me as hard as you can!"

***

Ajani pushed Stacey's knees to her chest and lined up his dick to meet her little hole. He moved his head in circles until her sex lips pursed out, then he slammed it home, falling in between her legs.

"Uhh! Yes! Yes, Daddy! Fuck me now! Fuck yo lil' baby now, Daddy!" She pulled her own knees apart further to help him.

Ajani didn't need no help, though, he got to running his dick in and out of her at full speed, while he sucked on her thick brown nipples. He sucked them as if she had milk in them and this drove her crazy and him in the process.

"Keep calling me, Daddy. I love that shit. Be my little girl. That's gon' make me kill this pussy!" he growled and went hammer on her ass.

Stacey felt his dick opening her up wider and wider every time he plunged into her pussy. She tried to suck him in further.

She could feel him in her stomach. "Fuck me, Daddy! Fuck yo, baby! Fuck me just like that! I love my daddy dick! I love it. I been saving this pussy for you Daddddeeeeee!" She started to shake uncontrollably.

The way her pussy started to clamp down on him Ajani couldn't help but to cum in huge globs, deep within her channel. Her pussy was so tight that it didn't allow for him to go soft.

He stayed hard and proceeded to fuck her with anger. He had to bite into her neck. "This my muthafuckin' pussy do you hear me, bitch? Huh? I'll body yo ass if you ever let another nigga get between these legs without my permission. Tell me you understand?" He pulled out and threw her on her stomach like a rag doll. "Tell me!" he hollered, grabbing a hand full of her hair.

Stacey loved getting fucked by a thug. The way he was treating her was making her fall in love. That was that savage shit that she needed. "It's yours, Daddy! It's yours. I will never let another nigga hit this pussy. It belongs only to my daddy."

***

Rayjon pulled out of Averie's pussy and let her guide his dick straight into her ass. She could hear the noises that her little cousin was making in the other room and she needed to one up her. She couldn't help but to feel jealous. She wondered if Ajani took the time out to think about her the whole time he was in Stacey, because even though Rayjon was putting it down she couldn't stop thinking about him.

Rayjon felt her asshole engulf his dick. It felt like it was back in her mouth all over again. He looked down at the way her back was arched, with her thick ass cheeks below it and couldn't help biting into his bottom lip. He grabbed her waist and stuffed his dick further into her bowels. It was a tight fit.

Averie bounced back into him with her eyes closed. She felt his pole reaching deep into her body and it felt good. She reached under them and played with her fat clitoris while he slapped her on the ass and fucked her harder and harder.

"Yes, Rayjon! Yes, baby! Fuck this ass! Fuck it just like that! Fuck me! I love this dick!" She felt him dig his fingers into her hips.

Rayjon pushed her head into the pillow and started to kill that ass. He was fucking her so hard and fast that it was hurting his abs. Her cheeks jiggled and shook. Rippling like brown waves. He never imagined that she was so strapped out of clothes. Her body was killing any stripper he had ever saw and not only was the pussy A-1, but so was her back shots.

"Give me this shit, Averie! Let big bro smash yo ass the right way."

He grabbed her swinging titties and used them for support. Her big nipples poked against the palms of his hands. He pulled them and that turned him on even more. He fell on top of her and pushed her right leg up to her ribs and really started to fuck her like crazy while she whimpered in ecstasy.

***

"You see, he just looked at me again. I think he recognize my face Aunty," Aiden said, eyeing the black dude from the corner of his eye. He was sure that he had been made.

He had killed the black dude's sister last summer because her baby daddy had paid him 10 G's to do so. He said the broad had him 50 thousand dollars in debt and her death would mean he wouldn't have to worry about constantly being locked up for failure to pay child support. He could get custody of their six kids and move on with his life.

Aiden didn't need all of the background. Long as the man paid him up front, which he did, he was good to go.

Jersey eyed the man from the corners of her eye. He sat two tables over with two little girls that didn't look like they were older than twelve. She already felt sorry for them because she knew that Aiden was going to kill their father, which she assumed the man was to them.

Marco had a bad feeling that he knew the weird looking light skinned nigga, with all the freckles over his face that kept on looking at him from the side of his face. He was sitting at the table with a caramel sista.

He felt strongly that he knew him from somewhere, he just didn't know where. He saw him get up to head to the rest room in the back and figured he'd follow him.

"Say look, I'm finna go use the bathroom. Y'all stay out here and finish y'all food. I'll be back in like ten minutes."

He got up and followed the yellow nigga before but pausing at the table where he'd previously sat with the sister.

Jersey saw him come over and look down on her. She sat back in her seat and put her hand in her Prada purse, immediately finding the .380 and placing it in her hand, outta sight. "Can I help you?"

Marco smiled. "Nall, unless you gon' give me yo number or something. I ain't never seen a sister as fine as you before. You are gorgeous."

She had to silently admit that he was handsome and the fact that he had a deep voice worked in his favor. But even if she wasn't happily married, he wouldn't have been her type. He was too short and didn't have enough muscles. She needed a goon.

A big ass nigga to make her feel small. And she needed him to be Greed and that he was not.

"Thank you for the compliment, baby. But I'm happily married."

Marco gave her a look that said he was in disbelief. "To homeboy in the bathroom?" He just knew that couldn't have been true. He felt like she could have done a whole lot better than him. He would have done anything for her to give him a chance.

"No, not to him. But I am married, so our words have to end here." She turned away from him and waved at the little girls at his table. Both were mixed and very pretty.

Marco felt defeated. He got the impression that she wasn't going for him and that he should give up. "Well, awright then, sister. Maybe I'll see you around."

Jersey smiled because she knew he wouldn't. "Yeah, but even then, I'll still be married, so…"

Marco walked away annoyed. He didn't know how to take the rejection. He wanted to get petty and say something slick but decided against it.

He pushed open the bathroom door and saw the yellow nigga washing his hands, and the first thing he saw was his wrinkled clothing. He looked dirty.

He couldn't see how the sister had let this dude in her presence. She was well put together. Rocking Prada from head to toe, he'd noticed.

It was a small bathroom with only two sinks and two stalls. There were three urinals and a big window up top along the far wall. It didn't smell too bad in there and for a bathroom in Los Angeles, it was fairly clean.

Marco walked up to Aiden and stood alongside of him. "Say, homeboy, don't I know you from somewhere? Ain't you…"

Aiden back handed him with the blade, slicing it across his face. Before the man could do anything, he faced him and sliced the blade across his neck sending blood splashing on to the mirror.

Marco grabbed his neck as he felt spurt after spurt of blood shoot out of his neck and ooze between his fingers. He started to choke on the fluid as he was being hoisted into the air.

Aiden carried him into the stall closest to the window, kicked open the door as quietly as he could, took Marco's head and stuffed it into the toilet.

"All you had to do is not look at me. Just keep eating your food. You're not even on my list for today, but you just had to jump on it. Yes, I killed your sister last summer. Yes, I look familiar because I stalked her for two weeks first and you saw me three times because I let you. Now you gotta die. Fuck, you have the worst luck."

The water went into his nose and mouth and mixed with the blood. He started gagging trying to breathe. Every time he tried to lift his head up, Aiden would push it further into the water.

His nostrils began to burn. His chest hurt. His lungs felt like he was breathing in nails. His heart was beating so fast that it was sure to burst. He kicked his legs and then he felt it.

He felt the worst pain he had ever felt in his entire life. He felt his lungs collapse. It felt like somebody had hit him in the chest with a sledge hammer and then parked a school bus right on top of him.

Before he knew, he was throwing up blood and all the fight had left out of him. The world faded to black.

Aiden pushed his head further into the toilet and then pulled him out. He sat him upright so that it appeared he was sitting on the toilet shitting. Blood continued to ooze from his wounds. He took a bunch of tissue and wiped away as much of the blood as possible from the mirrors.

After he cleaned up as much as he could, he climbed out of the window and broke down the alley where Jersey was waiting on him.

"You okay, baby?" she asked as he jumped into the truck and ducked down.

He nodded. "Yeah, I just need some ice cream. It's too hot outside. I just want some ice cream."

"Well, next stop is Baskin Robbins."

Chapter 13

Averie went to the back room and knocked on the door. It was three hours later and she was ready to be back in Ajani's arms. She didn't like imagining Stacey all hugged up with her man. Fucking was one thing, but all that cuddling shit was another.

"Ajani, I'm ready to come into my own damn room. Y'all been in there long enough!" She paused for a second to see what his response was going to be. After not hearing anything she twisted the knob and opened the door.

Stacey had his dick in her hand, kissing up and down it, as if she were worshipping it, while Ajani laid on his back going through his phone. The young girl made eye contact with her almost immediately and a little smile came across her face.

Averie felt her heart drop. She felt anger, frustration and jealousy all at once and that caused her to become enraged.

She shot toward the bed and grabbed Stacey by her natural curly hair, yanking her off of Ajani, after slapping her so hard it sounded like she had smacked her on the back instead of the face. "Bitch, now you doin' way too muthafuckin' much! Play time is over."

The blow to Stacey's cheek felt equivalent to being hit across the face with a big switch. It hurt so bad that tears started running down her face right away. "What the fuck is yo problem, Averie?

"You, bitch, but I'm finna change all that though." She rushed her and grabbed another handful of her hair, dragging her across the floor while she screamed.

"Ajani! Daddy, help me!"

He laid on the bed for a brief second feeling himself become hot. He figured that Averie wasn't going to be able to let shit ride. He felt that it was always somebody that had to ruin it for everybody else. He didn't care what she was feeling, he was going to keep fucking Stacey. Her pussy was fire.

Averie smacked her again, this time busting her lip. "I'm gon' teach you not to challenge me. You think this shit is all one big joke. Don't you, bitch?"

Stacey tried to shake her head, but Averie smacked her again.

Ajani jumped up and grabbed her around the waist and picked her into the air. He wasn't about to let her beat the shit out of the girl after all of them had sat down and agreed on what was to take place.

After all, she had just got down fucking his brother and he wasn't wilding out.

"Let me down, Ajani. I'm finna beat this bitch ass because I'm tired of her playing with me. She think all of this shit is a game not knowing that she fucking with my family. I ain't finna let this bitch break our shit up." She struggled to get back to Stacey's ass. All she wanted to do was to beat her for a little while. Just so she could get it through her head that playing with her man was unacceptable.

"Stacey go take a shower, lil' momma. Let me holler at yo big cousin and get an understanding. Go!" he ordered.

She slowly got up from the floor with her fingers to her lip, where it was bleeding. She walked slowly past them naked as the day she came into the world. She mugged the shit out of Averie. "You know you bogus for this. We all agreed and you couldn't handle it."

Averie wiggled in his grasp, trying to get him to drop her. "Oooh, let me get that bitch. Just let me get on her ass."

"Go shower, Stacey! And close that door behind you."

She followed his commands. Soon as the door was closed, she put her ear to it. She wanted to hear everything he was about to say to her. She couldn't see him breaking things off with her. After all, her pussy was young and fresh. He had been the only one to ever enter into it. There was blood on the sheets to prove that.

Ajani threw Averie onto the bed and stood in front of the door, just in case she tried to run out of it. "What the fuck is yo problem, huh?" He mugged her like she had lost her fucking mind.

She scrunched her face and struggled to get up from where he had thrown her on the bed. "I'm not the one with the problem. You are. How the fuck you gon' let this bitch be laying all in our bed sucking on your dick while I'm beating on the door trying to get into my own room? What type of shit is that?"

"We wasn't done. Ain't nobody set no time limits to this shit. I wasn't done getting' my dick sucked. Plus, I ain't buss up y'all party in there. So why you bussin' up ours? I was enjoyin' myself just like you was supposed to be. It ain't my fault that you wasn't." He was irritated.

How many niggaz gave their baby mommas the green light to fuck their brother? He felt she should have been appreciative. But instead there she was with a punk ass attitude. It almost made him want to slap her face to knock some sense into her.

Averie bounced out of the bed and almost stepped into his face but decided against it. She stood away at a safe distance.

"Oh, I definitely enjoyed myself. Every hole I got on my body hurt. That's why I was ready to come into my room and lay down. Had you just answered the door and told me y'all wasn't done, I would have walked away and got me some more. But nall you had to ignore me. Making it seem like this bitch was more important and I wasn't geeing for that."

Ajani felt like she was trying to shoot a shot at him a few moments ago so he decided to break her ass all the way down mentally. "In that moment, she was."

Averie felt her heart skip a beat. "Was what?"

"She was more important than you. Her pussy caught me off guard. I ain't know lil' momma was holding like that between her legs. But now I do and I gotta stay in that box. That's just how that's gon' go." He flopped down on the bed, and rested his head on his folded arms.

Averie stood their frozen. She blinked tears and felt so many emotions going through her all at once. The worst thing a woman that had a kid could hear come from her man was the fact that he desired a woman younger and more pure than her. All of her insecurities started to come rushing at her.

She knew there was no way she could compete with her little cousin. She was younger, prettier and until Ajani had taken it, was still a virgin. Her body didn't have any stretch marks. Her breasts had not went round after round with gravity as of yet and her womb had not pushed out a 6 pound baby.

She felt defeated. She slowly turned around and looked down on him.

"You know what, Ajani, I'm sorry, baby. I should have stayed in my lane. We did all sit on the couch and agreed to this. I should have kept my end of things. I didn't have no right putting my hands on that girl. I need to go apologize to her. Would that make you happy?"

She felt like shit. She felt like she could scream. She didn't mean a word that she was saying to him, but she had to say it. She had to make sure that they kept a strong foundation built around him. She couldn't raise their son on her own. He needed his father and so did she.

Ajani smiled. "Nall, you ain't gotta apologize. Just as long as you see where you were wrong, there shouldn't be any more problems after this." He saw that he had broken her down and there was no need to demoralize her by making her apologize to Stacey. "Come here, baby, and let me hold you."

As much as she hated his guts in that moment, she played the role of submissive woman. Crawled across the bed and laid her head on his chest. She was doing all that she could to not allow the tears to come out of her eyes. She had visions of killing him and Stacey.

In that moment, it would have made things so much easier.

He pulled her more firmly to him, rubbing her booty as she laid on her side. "There's one more thing that we gotta talk about, too." He patted her butt and squeezed a cheek.

He always liked how her ass felt. He couldn't deny that there was a distinct difference in comparison to Stacey's, but he liked them both, though he gave his baby momma the slight edge because her ass was fat.

She felt disgusted by letting him touch her. She was so mad that she wanted to physically hurt him. She needed to see him bleed. She wanted to cause him the same amount of pain he was causing her. "What do we need to talk about, baby?"

"Stacey. Now that we all know what it is, I wanna keep fucking with her on that level."

***

On the other side of the door, Stacey smiled. Things were getting juicy in there. She had been waiting for him to bring up the fact that they had decided for her to be his side bitch.

She didn't care how she was able to be a part of Ajani or what her role had to be because no matter what, she was all for it. She knew a few females that she kicked it with that were side bitchez and they were taken care of just as well as the main bitch in the house. Long as he kept piping her down and made sure she stayed fresh, she would play her role with no problems.

Rayjon came out of the bathroom and saw Stacey bent half way over with her ear to his brother's bedroom door. Her ass was perfect to him. She had her legs slightly spread and through her thigh gap, he could see her fat pussy. Bald and the lips on it open just a peek. He peeped her perfectly pedicured toes and the way her small breasts bounced on her chest and his dick got as hard as a gang banger. He crept up behind her.

Stacey licked her lips as she heard the argument ensuing.

Ajani was explaining to her why he thought it would be smart for her to be his side bitch. He was telling her that it was better that she knew who he was fucking instead of him being out there in the streets and fucking every bitch that could be burning with something. She was agreeing with him when she felt fingers part her sex lips, peeling them open ever so slightly.

She jumped and looked behind her.

Rayjon rubbed all over her booty. "I ain't even know you was holding like this, lil' cuz," he kept his eyes on her ass.

She looked over her shoulder at him and bit into her bottom lip. Quiet as it was kept, she had a thing for him, too. He was too fine to her and she liked his style because he was so laid back.

Now that he had the diamonds in his mouth it made him look that much finer. She popped back on her legs and spread them placing her ear back on the door, after putting one finger to her mouth to tell him to be quiet.

All Rayjon saw was that ass poked out, with that monkey from under it. He rubbed up and down her sex lips and slid his middle finger in her. When she didn't do anything other than moan, he took that as a sign to get serious.

Stacey felt him pushing his fat dick head into her box and she almost came. First one brother and now the other. It was turning into the best birthday ever. As he drove the full length of himself into her, she reached under herself and got to playing with her clitty.

***

"So now I'm supposed to just accept you fucking with her on a regular basis now? So where does that leave us?" Averie asked, sitting up in the bed.

She couldn't believe he had the audacity to come at her in the way that he was. She felt so disrespected and was getting ready to blow.

You still my son's mother. Me fucking her every now and then ain't gon' change that." He didn't really understand what the problem was. It wasn't nothing but fucking. After the sex was over, everybody could go on about their day. He just didn't want to be confined to one pussy. He felt that no man did.

Now Averie was really hurt. So, I'm just your son's mother, right? After all the work I done put in for our family, all I get is that title?" She shook her head and got out of the bed going straight into the closet to find something to wear. She's had enough. She was over that scene. She needed to find somewhere to breathe.

Ajani watched her as she started to get dressed. He shrugged his shoulders. He was tired and he didn't feel like arguing. He thought the only place she would go is to his mother's and they'd have their girl talk.

By the time he woke up, his mother would be calling him over to her house where she would play mediator between them. "I ain't got time for this shit. I know you better pick up my son before you go wherever you finna go."

Averie slid the boy shorts up her thighs and shook her head. She stepped into the Jordache jeans and buttoned them. Fixing her breasts inside of her bra, before throwing the blouse over her head. "The sad thing is that you don't even know how much I love you. You trample over me and treat me like I ain't shit not understanding that I am the mother of your child, but that I loved you way before he even came into this world. You're my everything, Ajani, and I'd do anything for you, other than allow you to destroy me. I'm not strong enough to handle the way you treat me. I deserve better." She slipped her foot into her Charles David's and tied them.

Ajani jumped up from the bed and blocked her path as she tried to open the door. He didn't want her to leave thinking he didn't care about her because that wasn't the truth.

"Averie, look, I'm sorry, baby. I ain't mean to make you feel like shit or nothing like that. I'm crazy about you and you know I'd body a nigga over you, with no hesitation. The shit I meant about Stacey was that I didn't think it was that big of a deal if I fucked her every now and then. It's better than me going behind your back and fucking wit another bitch. At least with her, you'll already know what's good. Everything would be out in the open." He prayed that she saw things his way.

To him she was over reacting. She was making things out to be more than what they were. He was seconds away from getting so irritated that he just gave up all together.

Averie blinked tears. "That's my little cousin, Ajani. I watched that little girl grow up. She has always respected me but now that she's able to fuck my man, she don't anymore and why should she?" She wiped her tears away. "I just expected more from you after all that we have been through. I never thought that another bitch would be able to move in on my slot like that. I would never submit to another nigga.

134

You're all I know. I just need to clear my head or if I don't I can't be responsible for what happens to that girl in there."

Ajani lowered his head. "Well, before you go, just know that I love you and we can work on this to make everybody happy. I'm willing to listen whenever you ready to have that sit down."

She nodded and bumped him as she walked out of the room.

Rayjon and Stacey were oblivious to what was taking place between Averie and Ajani. He had her bent over the washing machine fucking her so hard that her titties were slapping against her stomach. She had a drying towel in her mouth screaming muffled sounds at the top of her lungs with her eyes closed. Loving every minute of the assault.

Ajani plopped down on the bed and laid back, looking at the ceiling. He felt bad for hurting his baby mother. He knew she deserved better and it was his job to become a better man for her. He imagined if his father had done that to his mother where they'd all be.

He shook his head. "Fuck, I'm bogus, man. My Pops taught me way better than that." He jumped up out of the bed and threw his boxers on. He had to catch Averie before she left. He had to let her know that she was enough for him and their son.

Chapter 14

Game bent the corner in the cherry red Low Rider and flipped the switch so that it hopped up and down and then leaned to three-wheel motion. He hit the switch again and it hopped off of three-wheel motion and the front got to jumping up and down.

Behind him were four black vans and three Ducati's. He had been given the go ahead to handle business as he saw fit and he wanted to make a statement. As he turned on to Ajani's block, ready to wet his crib up, he couldn't believe his eyes as he saw Averie struggling to get into her Ford Explorer. He licked his lips like a cat that saw a wounded bird.

Averie slammed her fit against the truck's door. She hated the damn thing. It had this habit where it got stuck every now and then and that drove her crazy.

She put the key in the lock and tried to jiggle it inside in the hopes that it would pop open but it didn't and that frustrated her. She slammed her fist against it again. "Fuck, today is just not my day!"

As she was going to put the key in the back passenger's door she was mildly interrupted.

Game pulled up right next to Averie with a shotgun pointed directly at her. He had given the wheel of his car to Wacko and after dropping the top, he'd gotten into position. "Say, lil' bitch, long time no see."

When Averie turned around and saw what was taking place, she damn near had a heart attack. Her eyes got as big as sugar cookies. She dropped her Gucci bag and put her hands all the way in the air. "Please don't kill me, Game. Please, you know I got a son."

Game laughed and curled his upper lip. "What the fuck that got to do wit me? Bitch, I should blow yo head off right here. Stay still and don't move."

Tears sailed down her cheeks right away. All she could think about was her son and the fact that she might not ever get a chance to see him again. Now she wished she had never got into a petty argument with his father. She just wanted them to be back under the same roof.

She didn't even mind sharing him with Stacey any longer, just as long as she was a part of the equation.

Looney, jumped out of the van, ran over and put the black pillow case over her head. He picked her up in the air. and she started to scream at the top of her lungs.

Ajani made it as far as the porch and saw Looney pick his baby mother into the air. He thought about running toward the van when Game aimed the shotgun directly at him and fired.

Boom! Boom! Boom! Boom!

He knocked big chunks of wood out of the house. He went behind his back and pulled out a .45 automatic.

Boo-wa! Boo-wa! Boo-wa!

"Bitch ass nigga! Blood Bath, nigga!"

Boo-wa! Boo-wa! Boo-wa!

Ajani dropped to the ground and Rayjon stepped over him with the Mach. 90

Taaat! Taat! Taaat! Taaat!

He spit trying to knock holes into the black vans and Game's Low Rider. He watched as they started to scurt off down the street.

Game smacked the clip into his .45 and returned fire.

Boo-wa! Boo-wa! Boo-wa! Boo-wa!

Game saw Rayjon fall to the ground and he hoped that he had hit the man. He hated both of them with a passion and knew that it was about to jump off.

Rayjon got up off of the ground and jumped up and ran back toward Ajani. He had to make sure that his little brother had not been hit because he had not had the chance to check that before.

He had been solely focused on hitting the rival crew. When he got into the house, where Ajani retreated to weapon up, he was cocking back a Tech .9. He looked like he was ready to kill something. Rayjon saw he was about to run outside and he jumped into his way. "Bro, they gone. We gotta get the fuck out of here because you already know LAPD on they way."

Ajani lowered his head and tried to fight through him." Let me go man. Them bitch-niggaz got my baby momma. What the fuck am I gon' do?"

Rayjon held him. "Bro, I understand that but they not out there right now. We gotta develop a plan ad we gotta get the fuck out of here because you know 12 on they way. I ain't trying to be locked up. We can't handle shit from behind them walls. The only mafucka that navigate like that is Pops. We gotta get word to him ASAP."

Ajani fell to his knees. Tears streaming down his face.

He shook his head thinking over all the things that Averie had done for him and his son over the years. She was indeed an amazing woman. He hoped that the argument that they'd had wouldn't be the last time that he got to talk to her. He felt horrible.

***

Mollie came off of the basketball court and picked up his water bottle. He squirted the cool liquid over his face and took a deep breath. The sun was beaming like crazy. It felt like it was a million degrees outside. He grabbed the rest of his things and figured he'd get to the showers early before everybody else rushed into them from rec.

Greed made sure he turned the showers all the way up so there was so much steam that he could barely see in front of him. He had covered all bases.

He wanted to make a crucial statement to Suge, so he waited for his nephew to enter into the showers to get the ball rolling.

As soon as Mollie got naked, he slipped into the area where the shower heads were. Lucky for him, they were already turned on, which was unusual. The men ofen did that. They'd let the water run for thirty minutes prior 'til rec ended so that it wouldn't be so hot by the time they got into it.

Greed saw him come into the area, he nearly walked right past him but before he could, he took his blade and whipped it through the air, slicing him across the face deeply. So deep that his blade hit bone.

Mollie felt the stinging on his face and thought about screaming like a bitch because it hurt so bad. He was scooped into the air and dumped on his head. He felt his neck snap and then all along his back felt frozen. He tried to scream but no would come out.

Greed picked him up by his neck as the shower water beat on his back. He took his blade and stabbed him again and again, all in the neck, the face the chest and stomach. He stabbed him over a hundred times before leaving him there.

***

Game threw Averie into the empty bedroom so rough that she flew against the wall and landed on her stomach. He walked into the room and grabbed her up by her hair.

"Long time no see, bitch. I bet you wish you would have chosen me now, don't you?" He smacked her across the face.

Averie fell to the floor and scooted backward on her ass.

She didn't want any problems with Game. She remembered back in the day how he used to whoop her ass on a daily basis. "What do you want from me, Game? I haven't done anything to you. Your beef is not with me."

Game leaned down and smacked her again. "Bitch! Is that what you think? You think you ain't got nothing to do with this beef that I got going with these bitch ass niggaz?"

He picked her up by the hair and bumped his forehead against hers. "This shit got everything to do with you. Had you stayed in line, you would have still been my bitch and none of this shit would be happening."

There was a loud knock on the door. "Say, Game?"

He turned around in anger. "What the fuck do you want? Can't you niggaz see I'm busy in here?"

"Yeah, Blood, but we got the other thing you wanted us to snatch up," said the male voice through the door.

Game looked down on her and smiled. He released her hair and stood up.

That bitch actually kept up her end of the bargain, he thought to himself, referring to his connect Angela.

She was a straight hood bitch, who had owned the daycare facility Jahni had attended.

A few weeks prior, Game had given her an ounce of Loud in exchange for her assisting him with his mission.

Walking over to the door, he opened it and Averie saw her son pushed into the room. Game snatched Jahni up by his neck and held him in the air, closing the door with his other hand. "Here go Bitch Ass Nigga Jr."

Averie jumped up and rushed him. She attacked the arm that was holding her son in the air. "Let him go, Game. Please don't hurt my baby. He's just a child. Kill me but leave him alone." She tried with all of her might to pry Jahni loose.

Game went into the small of his back and brought out the .45. He put it to her Jahni's forehead. "Bitch, if you don't go sit yo monkey ass down, I'm blow this mini niggaz' head off." He growled praying that she didn't take heed to his advice because he wanted to kill the little boy for just looking like Ajani so much.

There was no doubt about it that he carried a sour taste in his mouth over how Ajani had taken Averie away from him. He still cared about her and was jealous that they had a son together. He always saw her coming back to him and when she didn't, he developed a strong hatred for Ajani and her. He couldn't help it.

Averie slowly walked backward with her hands in front of her, palms out. "Hey, Game, please don't hurt him. That's all I'm asking. He's just a baby and he's all that I have," she whimpered.

She could see her son was in pain because his little eyes were closed and his head was bent at a weird angle He had tears rolling down his cheeks and he cried as hard as he could.

Game put him down but kept the gun pointed at his head. "I want you to tell me who killed my baby mother? Which one of them niggaz did it? He frowned at her. "You can tell me what I want to know or I'm gon' waste this mini bitch-nigga."

Averie got on her knees and planted her forehead onto the ground. She felt like she was having a heart attack. She didn't know what the fuck Game was talking about. And now he expected her to tell him something or he was going to kill her son.

She started to hate life more and more.

"Who kilt my bitch and where is my money?"

***

As Midnight came through the cooler door, Greed scooped him into the air and slammed him against the section of frozen Hot Dogs. The big 300 pound, black man was taken off guard. He tried to gather himself but Greed swung and hit him in the jaw so hard that it shattered. It felt like his face was melting and then the pain started.

"Bitch ass nigga. You mafuckas wanna play games wit my family out there. Okay then?" He scooped Midnight into the air and dumped him on his head. Knelt down and got to stabbing him in the face again and again. "Where the fuck is my daughter, Averie? Where is my grandbaby? Why are you niggaz testing my gangsta? Don't y'all know that I live for this shit?"

He stabbed him again and again. His blood spurt into the air and it didn't bother him one bit. This was Suge's right hand man. He was second in command all throughout California. But that shit didn't mean nothing to Greed. He felt like he was back in his Ski Mask Cartel days. The days where killing came at a price.

Just as he was standing up from killing Midnight, Kevlar was thrown into the cooler by Lox. Greed grabbed him by the throat and put the blade to his face. Smoke came from his nose and mouth because they were ducked off in the freezer way in the back of the main kitchen. It was ten below zero inside of it, but to Greed it felt like it was 100 degrees.

Kevlar felt like he was ready to shit on himself. He had thought about not showing up for work that day and he felt he should have went with his first mind. Now Greed had him in the air by his neck and he had piss dripping out of his dick.

"I need to know where the fuck my shorties at, nigga? Where the fuck Game lil' duck off?" Greed could feel his heart pounding in his chest. He had an addiction for killing. Once he started, it was often hard for him to stop.

Kevlar swallowed and pissed so more. "He got a pad over on Normandy and Center. Every time we used to hit licks back in the day, that's where we'd take our vics until they told us what we needed to know. Then we'd stank they ass and bury them in the cemetery three blocks over. He got a plug with the grave digger over there."

Greed flung him against the wall. He pulled back out the blade and chased him down because he tried to shoot out of the door, not knowing that Lox was on the other side making sure that nobody came out or went in.

Many palms were greased for the time limits, but it was necessary. He brought the blade down in his back and pulled downward slicing him open all the way to his kidney.

Once there, he raised the knife and slammed it right into his kidney. The little organ splattered and he stabbed it again and started to dig it out.

Kevlar flopped around like a fish on his stomach. He was in so much pain. Blood spurt from the head of his dick and came out of his nose. He tried to say something but only coughed up a loogey of blood.

Greed, stabbed the blade into his back again and trailed it downward until he got to the other kidney. Once there, he scooped it out and placed them in a bag. He knocked over a bunch of frozen food and left out of the cooler after knocking three times.

***

"Game, I swear to you that if I knew anything I would tell you everything. There is nothing going on in my life that would make me choose it or my baby. He is my everything."

She was crying so hard by this point that she felt like she was getting ready to pass out. She kept on imagining him killing Jahni and it was taking her breath away.

Game dropped the little boy to the ground and watched him run to his mother. He fell and got back up, running until he was safely in her arms.

As much as he wanted to cause her and Ajani pain, he didn't know if he had it in him to actually kill their child. That was a little more gangsta than what he had in him. To kill a kid, one had to be heinous, was what he figured, and he wasn't really there yet. He could kill her with no problem, but a baby was another thing altogether.

"You need to listen to me, Averie, because I'm not playing. I'm about 99 percent sure that I'm gon' kill you. I mean I'm gon' blow yo muthafucking head off if you don't tell me what I need to know because I know y'all pillow talk. That nigga driving a brand-new Bentley. Got a red-faced Rolex on his wrist. You had to ask him where he got all of that shit from and he had to jack on my name and tell you. All I'm asking is that you tell me what he said and you can go about yo business free as a bird, after I fuck you. Because I'm definitely doing that. You done got way too thick." He licked his lips. "I bet that shit still good, too, ain't it?" He made a disgusted face.

She hugged her son more firmly to her chest. She wasn't concerned about him getting on top of her. She just hoped that he used a condom. She was more concerned about him being at 99 percent on killing her. Then she started to think about Ajani, the new car he was rocking, along with the jewelry.

She wondered if he had bodied Game's baby momma in order to come up with everything. She remembered asking and him not telling her anything. But that's how it always went. He never told her about anything that he did in the streets. He always said he didn't feel that it was her business.

"Game, all I know is that when I asked him about the new car and stuff, he said he'd been saving for a while. He didn't tell me anything else and if he had, you would have known that already. We don't have that kind of pillow talk. The things we talk about revolve around our son. His street business is his business and I don't ask him to inform me."

Snot tried to sneak out of her nose but she sniffed it back up. Her son was crying beneath her and on top of that she had to piss worse than ever.

Game looked down at her thick thighs and felt his dick harden. When they had been together she wasn't as thick. It seemed like after she had the kid, her body filled out in all of the right places.

He believed she was telling the truth, but he wasn't about to let her know that. "You know what, shorty? I don't believe you. I feel like you hidin' something from me and I'm gon' get it out of you one way or the other." He crouched down and squeezed her thigh. "You want me to have my nigga come in here and snatch up yo son before I hit this pussy or you don't mind if he watch? Me personally, I can go either way."

***

Greed sat back on the bleachers and shielded his eyes from the sun. It was hot as hell outside and the prison staff had called a heat advisory, which meant that nobody could work out without the prison staff stopping them. Greed always hated those times because he felt like he was being chastised. He didn't like nobody telling him what to do or how to do it. He had always been a Boss. A mafucka that figured things out ahead of time and called the shots.

Lox stepped forward and looked out into the rec field. "Say, Chief, here come them punk ass Blood Bath niggaz. You want us to start poking shit?" He put his hand under his shirt ready to pull out the 11-inch blade that he'd sharpened last night.

He wanted to poke one of those niggaz. He felt like it would take away his depression. He had been plugged under Greed since before his old man died.

His old man ran under Greed's Ski Mask Cartel back in the day. A flamboyant man that kept him and his family eating good at all times. Before his old man passed away from liver disease, he told him to pledge his loyalty to Greed, and that's just what he had done. Even though he was in prison, his family never wanted for anything. That was all because of his big homie.

Greed slid the dark shades across his face to shield his eyes from the sun. He saw the Bloodz coming, over about ten deep. He noted that Suge was in the middle of the pack and it looked like he had chosen the biggest niggaz he could find to walk with him.

As soon as they got close to the dip bars, about 15 cartel members stood up and blocked their path. Greed curled his lip.

Suge walked to the front of the pack. "Yo, Greed, I need to holler at you man to man, Blood."

Greed could see the big handle sticking out of his shirt and that only excited him.

Chapter 15

"Let him through, but keep the rest of them niggaz at bay. Mafucka even look stupid, we sendin' this bitch up," he hollered, looking Suge in the eye.

Suge came through the pack of wild niggaz and mugged every last one of them. It wasn't no secret that he was as much of a goon as every one of them. There wasn't no way that one could get to his position and not have that straight cold hearted killer's mentality. His body count ran from California all the way to New York. He'd put in work in nearly 40 something states.

Greed met him half way and stepped into his face. "What's good, nigga?" He clenched his jaw off and on and tried to restrain himself.

He hated the Blood niggaz. Not because he was a Blood but in his mind, he was a straight bitch-nigga that hid behind his organization.

Greed was a killer without his Cartel. When it came to getting his hands dirty, he ain't have no problem getting down. But Suge always sent other niggaz to do his jobs for him.

Suge looked up at the bigger monster and flared his nostrils. "You kilt my nephew, nigga?"

"In cold muthafuckin' blood. Bodied his bitch ass and I ain't through." Greed was ready to grab his blade and slice the fat nigga up. He ain't like all that talking shit. He felt that real goons proved who they were by actions.

Suge nodded his head. "So that's where you wanna take shit, huh?" He wiped his mouth. "You really think that I'm about to rollover and accept that shit, nigga?"

Greed bumped forehead with him. "Bitch nigga, make yo next move yo best move."

He pushed his forehead away with his own and took a step back. "Now I need to know where my daughter and my grandson being kept. If you can't tell me that, shit gon' get a lil' uglier for you and you know I'm not really that nigga that make empty threats."

Suge mugged him as evil as he possibly could. He wanted his breath taken out of his body. He felt the world would be a better place for all Chiefs if Greed was no longer on the planet.

The man didn't honor anything or anybody and it drove him crazy. "Look, man, I'll send word out there for that situation to cease and desist. But in return you gotta tell me who snuffed my son's baby mother and brothers. We also had a lot of product come up missing. I want at least half of our shit back." He really didn't like making deal with Greed because he didn't think the man had a loyal bone in his body outside of his organization. But he figured if they were going to release his son's baby mother and their child, that he was going to get something for it.

The fact that Suge had just admitted he had knowledge about Averie's kidnapping along with his grandson's was enough to make Greed lose his mind. Before he could even think about the consequences, he pulled his fist back and brought it forward with so much velocity that when the punch connected with Suge's nose, it broke it in three places.

It shattered the bone underneath his skin and fractured both cheeks. He fell backward in what seemed like slow motion and Greed went nuts, beating his body up with blow after blow. By the time he hit the ground, he had so many broken bones it was ridiculous.

The Bloodz pulled out their shanks and started swinging them crazily. Greed's cartel was ready for the war play because they pulled out shanks that looked like mini swords. After Greed dropped Suge, he started to stomp him again and again, then he pulled Lox to him. "Y'all fuck these niggaz over. I can't get caught in this riot. You know what I'm on."

Lox nodded and watched Greed as he took off running into the building at full speed.

***

Game picked Averie up and threw her on the bed. He had just made her take a shower so she was smelling fresh and clean. He closed the door behind him and told Wacko to not knock on the door unless it was an emergency.

Averie scooted back on the bed to try and get as far away from him as possible. The little short gown that he had given her to wear barely covered anything. Every time she moved it went up around her waist, making her reveal her naked sex.

She was worried about her son. Game made him lie down on the floor and told him not to move.

Game took his black wife beater off, revealing a rock hard body full of tattoos. He grabbed the remote control off of the dresser and turned on the R. Kelly album.

To him, it wasn't nothing like fucking to Kells. If he could, he would have a mansion just like the man where all kinds of young bitchez would worship him just because he was a Boss.

He pulled down his boxers and started stroking his dick. "I'm 'bout to hit that pussy for old time sake. Do me a favor and open them legs up."

Averie scooted back further on the bed. She glanced at the floor to make sure her son was okay. After confirming he was, she took a deep breath and opened her legs.

Game smiled and stroked his dick faster. "Damn that mafucka done got fat," he said, noting the way her pussy lips had swelled up since the last time he saw her. Her shit looked like a mini brown booty. It was super juicy. "Open them lips for me and let me see that pink."

Averie felt humiliated. Not only did she hate this man guts but he was taking advantage of her. And he was doing it while her son was in the room. That was the ultimate slap in the face.

She put her hand between her legs, took two fingers and opened up her sex lips for him to peer inside of her.

Game started to shiver. "That's that shit I'm talking about. Now tell me that you like playing wit yourself in front of me. I want you to act like we back in the ninth grade and you still my little girlfriend. I'm know I'm older than you and shit, but so what. Talk to me and call me Daddy. Every nigga love that shit."

Averie felt ready to break down. He was simply asking way too much of her. She didn't think she could fulfill all that he wanted. She just wished he would jump on top of her and do his business.

At least then the act would be over and done with.

"Game, can we just get on with it. I don't want to do all of that," she whimpered.

"Bitch, if I have to grab that gun off the dresser, I'm gon' kill yo kid. Now do like I ask you." He stroked his dick. "Call me Daddy and tell me how much you love to play with yo lil' ninth grade pussy. You used to do it all the time, you remember?"

Averie took a deep breath and tried to calm herself down.

Jahni picked his head up and looked directly at her. "Mommy, I want my daddy," he whined. "I don't want to put my head down like this. It's roaches under there."

Game flew around the bed and pushed the little boy's face into the carpet. "You micro bitch nigga, keep yo head in the floor or else I'ma stomp yo lil' ass. Now we could have been done wit this shit but yo punk ass momma playing games."

"Okay, Daddy, I'm sorry. I'll be a good girl. I'll do everything you say. Just tell me what you want me to do."

***

Greed heard the alarm bell going off indicating that all officers were to report to a certain location.

"All first responders please report to the rec field. I repeat! All first responders please report to the rec field!" The person blared across the speakers.

He ran full speed until he got to the North Cell Hall. As soon as he got there, he ran to cell B-31. Kabir was just coming out of it.

As they nearly bumped into each other, about fifteen Arab men pulled out their shanks ready to rush Greed, but Kabir held up his hand and they paused in their tracks.

"What's the matter, brother?"

Greed spoke on cue. "I know you got people in high places that's across them waters. I need for you to do me a favor. I know that you're hot and they can't really move on your behalf but have them move on mine and when I hit them bricks, your enemies will become my enemies. And I'll get you home no matter what I gotta do."

Kabir looked him up and down. "Would you be willing to travel beyond this country, if need be? I mean, to very dangerous places with men that are as crazy as you are? If you are, then I can help you and I can make you a very rich man. Just take care of one list for me. That will get me home, and I can claim my throne."

Greed didn't care what the man asked of him or who he had to body. He was all for it. The world was no match for him and his sons when he stood atop them as the head. His family was his number one concern.

Chapter 16

Boom!

The door fell off of the hinges as Rayjon kicked it in with all of his might. He upped the Tech .9 and started bussing.

Baba-locka Baba-locka Baba-locka Baba-locka!

The bullets ripped into the teenager's face who was sitting on the couch playing his video game. His brain splashed on to the wall behind him. Rayjon looked further into the house and saw about four dudes in the living room start to scatter. He dropped down to his knee and let the Tech spit.

Baba-locka! Baba-locka! Baba-locka!

They started to fall all over each other. He ran to where they were, finishing them off. Brains and blood shot into the air and all over his all-black outfit.

He heard screaming in the room to the left of him. He bust through it with his shoulder and saw a female in the bed with a sheet wrapped around her. She looked like she was Mexican or something Spanish.

"Please don't kill me. Please! I'm begging of you," she whimpered.

"Where the fuck is that nigga, Game. I heard he be all through this spot, bitch!" He aimed the Tech directly at her ready to pull the trigger. "Tell me!"

"I don't know. I swear to God I don't know. The last time he was over here was two days ago. I haven't seen him ever since then."

Rayjon shook his head. "Damn, that's fucked up." He pulled the trigger and splattered her brains all over the room.

He was in the state of mind where it was no mercy. It was all about bloodshed. Mafuckas was playing wit his nephew and his moms and that shit wasn't about to fly.

***

Jersey took the blow torch and put it up against Joanne's cheek, then she started the fire. Turning it slightly, she burned a hole into her face and heard the woman scream her head off.

"Bitch, I know you know where your son is keeping my grandbaby. Now I ain't got time for this bullshit that you spitting. I'm gon' show you how we get down in the Edwards' family." She took the torch and burned a hole directly into her forehead.

It smelled like cooked bacon in the room.

Joanne felt the flame heating up the skin on her forehead and nearly passed out. She screamed at the top of her lungs and tried to beg for mercy.

She didn't know how Jersey could do her like that when they sang in the choir right beside each other every Sunday morning. All she wanted for her was to take the duct tape off of her mouth so she could tell her where her son was.

She had to let him go. It wasn't her job to protect him any longer.

Jersey burned a hole in the back of her neck. She watched her skin bubble up and then it popped. Blood seeped down her spinal cord.

"All I want is my grandbaby and his mother back. I'm not asking for too much. I go to church every Sunday. Me and my family don't mess with nobody's kids unless we have to. Now my boys told me they didn't have nothing to do with your son getting hit. But y'all still came at us with that dumb shit. Knocked my baby's teeth out. Then had the nerves to shoot at them. You muthafuckas could have killed one of my kids. Mine! It took me over 36 hours to bring both of them into the world and who the fuck do you think you are to try and take them out in minutes? Tell me what's yo problem, bitch! Now!" She ripped the tape off of her mouth.

"Ahhhhhh! Why are you doing this to me? I don't deserve this. I have nothing to do with what my son do…"

Jersey slapped the shit out of her with the blow torch and she fell right on her back, still taped to the chair but knocked out cold.

Aiden picked her up from the cold floor of the cabin. He picked up the bucket of ice cold water and threw it into her face.

Joanne awoke with a startled look. She took a huge deep breath and opened her eyes wide.

"I'm gon' ask you one more time. Where the fuck is my grand baby?"

Joanne started crying and whimpering. "They're at his father's old house in Winsor. The address is on S. Deforest Drive. It's the first bricked building on the left. You can't miss it."

Aiden smiled. "Well, that's all we need to know." He picked her up and carried her into the back yard where he threw her into a double sized metal tub and then doused her with gasoline.

Jersey pushed him to the side and lowered the flame of the torch onto her, igniting her. "Burn in hell, you punk bitch. This what happens when you fuck with my family."

Joanne felt the fire shoot all over her body. The heat spread like the worst rash known to man. She tried to. jump out of the metal basin, but Jersey swung a bat and connected with her forehead knocking her back down inside of it.

"Aaaaa! Aaaah! Help me! Help me! Somebody please" She screamed into the woods.

She could feel her skin slowly bubbling and melting away. The pain was so bad that she prayed God would take the life out of her body.

Aiden took the gasoline and poured more onto her, making the flames shoot into the air.

Every time she tried to jump out of the basin, Jersey would slam the bat into her back or forehead.

Aiden stood back watching his Aunty in amazement because seeing her in action made him feel normal.

***

Ajani cocked back and punched the woman in the nose with all of his might, causing blood to spurt across his mask. He threw her to the floor and put the steel to her baby father's head. "I'm gon' ask you one more time, Kelly. Where the fuck is my baby mother and son at? I need an address right the fuck now or I'm splashing yo baby daddy and I know this nigga just getting home for doing a stretch that you held him down for."

August picked her up by the hair and yanked her head backward. He hadn't been back in town for two hours before he was forced to handle business alongside his cousin. It was the best welcome home present he could ever get. He, like his big brother, Aiden, lived for bloodshed. It was the main thing that kept the both of them sane.

Kelly felt him yank her head back so far that it snapped slightly and caused a horrible pain to shoot down her spinal cord. She felt her toes go numb. "He's at my dad's house over on Deforest. Please just leave us alone. We don't have anything to do with that stuff that he has going on."

August looked up at Ajani for approval. "You believe this bitch?"

Boo-wa!

Gary's brain exploded and jumped out the back of his head. It felt like he'd been hit by a car right in the forehead.

158

He fell onto his back in the living room of his baby mother's crib.

For a brief second, he watched the ceiling fan spin around and around before the masked Ajani stepped over him and sent fire from his gun. The bullets ate into his face and continued to knock the rest of his brain out.

"Ahhh! Ahhh! Why would you kill him? What have you done? What have you done?" Kelly screamed.

August took two fist fulls of her hair and yanked her head back so far that it completely snapped. He stood up, with his back to hers and yanked her hair over his shoulder and fell to his knees, pulling forward. With all of his might, he did it again and again until she stropped squirming.

When Kelly felt him grab a hold of her hair, she started to panic because of how aggressive he did it. The next thing she knew she felt this incredibly pain in her neck and the sound of her bones snapping. Her whole body went numb, but she could see everything still.

He then yanked her head backward again and again, then laid her on the floor and twisted it around on her neck until a huge bone popped out the side of it and everything went black.

Chapter 17

Game climbed from between Averie's thighs and stood up yawning. "Uhhhaw." He stretched his hands over his head. "Damn, baby, you still got that fire cat. That shit still tight even though you popped out that big head lil' nigga right there. Science a mafucka." He shook his head as he looked down at her.

She was curled into a ball on her side. She had tears on her face and she was shaking uncontrollably. He wondered what her problem was because things could have been a lot worse.

"Say, bitch, what the fuck is wrong with you? Why you in this mafucka crying and shit like I just kilt you or something? Do you know I could have bodied you and that lil' nigga right there?" He scrunched his face and got so irritated that he was again thinking about killing her.

Averie swallowed. "I just feel a little sick that's all. It don't have nothing to do with you. I know you could have killed me and my son and I thank you for not doing that." Averie felt like complete shit.

Not only had Game raped her in front of her kid, but now she had to stroke his ego in order for them to keep their lives. She wondered what it all meant. Why had life dealt her such a bad hand?

"I was finna say, because all I did was take the pussy. I mean yo nigga kilt my baby mother and her two brothers, so I could have easily bodied you and that micro bitch nigga right there." He pointed at Jahni.

The little boy was all cried out. He wondered why the man had been on top of his mother. He knew he wasn't his father and that it was wrong.

Now his mother cried and that made him cry. He just wanted to go home. He wanted to see his father because he would make things all better.

"So when are we getting out of here?" Averie asked him, sitting up in the bed. She wanted to pick his brain somewhat.

She had to know what was going on inside of it. She knew Game wasn't too bright. He always exposed his hand sooner or later.

"He snickered. "Leaving? Bitch, after the way I just piped you down, you still wanna go back to that nigga?" He looked at her like she had lost her mind. He was thinking that he'd fuck her at least fifty more times. All the times that he had not been able to because she had chosen Ajani over him. In his head, she had a whole lot of making up to do. "You stayin' with me for a long time, Averie. You might as well get used to this room because you gon' be here for a while."

He reached into the dresser and pulled out a pack of Newport shorts, taking one out of the pack and lighting it, inhaling deeply. "The way I see it, yo baby daddy kilt my baby mother, so instead of me killing you, bitch, I'm just gon' keep you on lock. We gon' transfer you out to the warehouse later on today when it stop all that mafuckin' raining. You see this shit?"

He pulled back the curtain to show her how dark it was outside and how hard the rain was coming down. "It been like this for days. They got people out there swimming in the middle of the streets. Lucky you in here with me safe and sound, huh?"

Averie wanted to throw up. She couldn't believe Game's sick sadistic ass had thoughts of keeping her in some warehouse where he could take advantage of her again and again. She wondered what was really going on in his head.

"What about my son, Game? You didn't say nothing about him. Where is he going to be?"

He shook his head and blew the smoke out. "Yeah, I ain't trying to be taking care of no other nigga's kid, so I gotta stank lil' dawg. He looked needy as a mafucka, too. I'm gon' be on top of his momma so much that it ain't gon' be no time to be caterin' to his lil' punk ass needs." Game mugged the lil' boy.

He figured he'd drown him in the bath tub or something quick like that.

Every time he saw him, he basically saw Ajani's face and that irritated him.

His intentions caused Averie to shudder. She jumped from the bed and fell to the floor wrapping her arms around her son protectively. She was crying so hard that she couldn't see straight.

"Don't hurt my child, Game. I've given you all of me. Everything that you have asked of me, I've given you. Please don't hurt him."

He shrugged his shoulders. "I don't like lil' boys. Maybe if he was a girl or something we could find a way to make shit work, but he ain't, so that's fucked up. I'ma let you say yo final goodbyes, then I'ma be back to kill that micro nigga. Don't try and put him through the window because there's bars on them, so that'll be a waste of time." He knocked on the door four times. It opened and he stepped out.

Averie broke down worse than she had ever before. She didn't know what to do. She shot up and opened the window just as the lightning flashed across the sky, followed by a roar of thunder.

Boom!

She could feel the rain and cool air coming in from the window and as much as she hated thunder storms, she would have given the world to be in it at that time along with her son.

She tried the bars on the window, but they were solid. There was no escaping from that way.

"Pow. Pow. Pow. Mommy, I want to shoot that man with that," Jahni said from behind her.

She continued to shake the bars to see if they would loosen even a little bit. The more she confirmed they would not, caused the tears to flow heavily down her face. "What is life?" she whimpered. She wondered where Ajani was and if he was even looking for them? Or was he somewhere laid up with Stacey enjoying her body?

"Pow. Pow. Pow. Mommy, I wanna shoot that big man with that right there," Jahni repeated.

Averie turned around and looked down on him. "What are you talking about, baby?" She rubbed his handsome face, and once again the tears fell from her eyes.

Jahni walked over to the dresser and pointed to the top of it. "That Pow Pow right there. I want to shoot it at him to leave us alone."

Averie's heart started beating so fast she could barely breathe. She reached to the dresser and grabbed the .9 milli-meter from off of it. It felt heavy in her hands. She checked the bottom of it and popped the clip out and slammed it back in like Ajani had taught her.

Cocking it back, she tilted her head toward the ceiling and said thank you to the Lord above.

***

Rayjon pulled down the block from the house that Game's mother had confirmed he was at. He mugged it with hatred. He couldn't believe that the fuck nigga had the balls to keep trying their family like it was sweet or something.

He prayed he would be able to get his hands on him. He wanted to kill him without the use of a bullet. Bullets were fast and made a person bypass all the pain they should have been forced to endure. That was something Rayjon's father had always told him. He said whenever he got the chance to kill an enemy with bare hands, do it. Make them suffer so that their soul never changes over. Tortured souls were incapable of crossing over to paradise.

"I wanna fuck this nigga over, big bro. I ain't never wanted to kill a nigga the way I do him," Ajani said, cocking back his Mach .90. He tapped the trigger to make sure the green beam was enacted.

The rain beat down heavily on the pizza delivery van that Aiden had brought them. They didn't know where he got it from and they didn't ask.

Aiden mugged the house. "I'm ready to go and have some fun. Let's make a statement before we leave L.A."

***

Game finished getting dressed and took one last look at himself in the mirror. He ran his hand over his waves and cheesed his teeth together. "I gotta get these muthafuckas cleaned next week or something." He hated that he had developed a habit of smoking cigarettes. It made it so hard to keep his grill in order.

He thought about brushing his teeth again but then decided against. He had to kill the little boy, even though he didn't like murdering children. But this lil' nigga was a whole 'notha case. He was the seed of the mafucka he despised.

Yeah, I'ma stank his little bitch ass and then I got to get Averie over to the warehouse before my next shipment of cocaine comes in, he smiled and thought to himself that as soon as he was done handling his business, he was going to hit that pussy one more time before he called it a day.

He stepped out of the bathroom and into the hallway. After taking the master lock off of the door, he opened it and stepped in.

Averie was sitting on the bed holding her son. She looked up at him with tears in her eyes. "Please don't tell me that you came in here to kill him."

Game shrugged his shoulders. "It's time. I already told yo we can't keep his lil' bitch ass with us. I ain't for taking care of no other nigga kids. That shit just ain't in me. Never have been." He snatched Jahni out of her arms by his shirt.

"Nooo! Let me go! I'ma tell my daddy on you." The little boy whined.

Game mugged the shit out of him. "Nigga, fuck yo daddy, lil' nigga." He put the little boy's back to his chest, then he wrapped his arm around his neck, almost as if he were putting the little boy in a sleeper hold. As soon as he had him positioned the way he wanted him to be, he started to choke the life out of him. "Yo, Averie, this shit ain't even gon' hurt him. He gon' be dead in no time."

Jahni kicked his little legs and tried his best to get free but to no avail. He couldn't breathe and he was getting more scared by the second.

Averie jumped up from the bed and slammed the gun to Game's head, surprising the fuck out of him. "You betta let my son go right now, nigga, or I'ma pull this trigger and kill you." She forced it more firmly into his temple. "I'm not playing with you. Let him go!" Tears fell from her eyes and her heart was pounding so hard that she could hear it in her ears.

Game was paralyzed for a few seconds. He didn't understand where she had gotten the gun from until it clicked in his mind.

He remembered that before he had fucked her, he'd put the gun on the dresser thinking he was going to slip it under the pillow, but he'd forgotten to do so. Now, Averie had him in a fucked up predicament. But Game refused to show fear.

"Oh, you 'bout that life?" He chuckled.

"Try me." Her voice was shaky but her trigger finger held steady.

"Try you?" He paused. "Bitch, maybe I will."

Game let Jahni drop to the floor. It was *do or die* time for him and Averie, as the dark cloud of death seeped into the room, ready to claim one of them.

***

Jersey ran out of the rain and up to the door. She beat on it for a few seconds and took a step back. Behind her it was pouring. Thunder boomed in the distance and every so often, lightning would flash across the sky.

She was ready to watch her sons murder some shit. She hoped they had been given a credible tip.

Fax walked to the door and looked out of the peep hole. He could see a female in a rain coat. Shaking as if she was freezing cold. He figured it was probably one of the homegirls from around the way. He took the two by four from across the door and the chains, then he opened it and took a step back.

Mistaking Jersey for someone else, he said, "You betta get yo as in here before you get struck by lightning. Game is in the back, he'll be out here in a few."

Jersey looked passed him and pulled the hood tighter around her head. She could see there were at least eight other men inside with red rags draped around their necks. She took a second and text what she saw to her oldest son.

She walked further into the house but before he could close the door behind her, Aiden ran up on the porch and put a shotgun right under Fax' chin and pulled the trigger.

Booooom!

Fax' scalp detached from his head and his brains shot up and hit the ceiling.

Jersey fell to the floor and rolled to the side of the couch and stayed down. She saw the men in the other room begin to scatter. "What the fuck?" One of them screamed like a surprised bitch.

"This is *what the fuck!*" Ajani came through the doorway bussing his twin .45's.

Boo-wa! Boo-wa! Boo-wa! Boo-wa! Boo-wa! Boo-wa!

His bangers was folding niggas up, one after the other.

Three bodies hit the floor, lifeless. Two niggas avoided the onslaught and whipped out their pieces, while half running and ducking behind furniture. Almost simultaneously, they spun around and blasted back. But their aims were rushed and errant, and their combatants' aims were precise.

Splacka! Splacka! Splacka! Splacka! Splacka! Splacka!

Aiden and Ajani let loose a succession of deadly gunfire, chopping the boys.

Quickly, Aiden ran over to the tattered pair. One of the niggas was still alive. He had dropped his strap, and now he was crawling on his knees to retrieve it as blood leaked from his bullet riddled body.

"Where the fuck you think you're going?" spat Aiden, rhetorically. He kicked the boy in the side with force, knocking him flat on his face.

"Don't kill me, man," the boy cried.

"Nigga, you already dead!"

Splacka! Splacka!

Aiden put him down permanently with two shots to the back of the dome.

Behind him, Ajani was crunk. "Where the fuck my baby momma at? And where is my son?" He barked at the last two men who were still alive and breathing. Both of them were bleeding profusely but that bought neither of them any mercy from the killer that stood over them.

"Oh, y'all niggas wanna play hard?" He pressed his gun directly against the forehead of the one closest to him.

Boom!

Blood and brains sprayed out of the man's head and his body instantly went still.

"Averie! Averie! Where you at, shorty?" He yelled and aimed his guns at the back of the other one. He was done asking for their assistance.

Boo-wa!

The man's back opened up in a splatter of red.

Before that mafucka could stop shaking, August came behind him, slicing the man's throat, causing his blood to spurt across the carpet.

Ajani stepped over the corpses and went to search for his girl and his son.

"Averie! Baby, where are you?" He prayed that she and his son were still alive.

***

Ajani's voice distracted Averie for a split second, and that's all it took for Game to flip things back in his favor.

As soon as she turned her head, Game hit her with a lightning quick backhand.

Whap!

Stunned by the impact, Averie's knees buckled.

Whap! Whap!

Game's hand was a blur.

The gun slipped from Averie's grip and fell to the floor as her ears rang.

Game scooped her into the air, dumping her on her back. "Punk ass bitch!" The gun slid across the floor.

Though dizzy, Averie knew she had to reach it before he did or else her and her baby, who was balled up in a corner, terrified, would surely be killed. She searched for it with her eyes and located it up against the far wall.

Game's eyes saw what hers saw, as well, and they both dove for the gun at the same time.

Seconds later, the door came crashing in.

Game wasn't fazed. He had recovered the banger. He looked up and saw Rayjon in the doorway aiming a Mach .90 directly at him.

A psychotic smile crept across Game's face as he pointed his tool squarely at Rayjon's chest.

Rayon smiled back at that nigga.

Neither man flinched.

"Let's do this shit!" They both said at the same time.

To Be Continued...
Bloody Commas 2
Coming Soon

Stay Connected with Us!

Text **LOCKDOWN** to 22828 to stay up-to-date with new releases, sneak peaks, contests and more…

Thank you!

BOW DOWN TO MY GANGSTA

By **Ca$h & Jamaica**

TORN BETWEEN TWO

By **Coffee**

BLOOD OF A BOSS **IV**

By **Askari**

BRIDE OF A HUSTLA **III**

THE FETTI GIRLS **III**

By **Destiny Skai**

WHEN A GOOD GIRL GOES BAD **II**

By **Adrienne**

LOVE & CHASIN' PAPER **II**

By **Qay Crockett**

THE HEART OF A GANGSTA **II**

By **Jerry Jackson**

TO DIE IN VAIN **II**

By **ASAD**

LOYAL TO THE GAME **IV**

By **T.J. & Jelissa**

A DOPEBOY'S PRAYER **II**

By **Eddie "Wolf" Lee**

A HUSTLER'S DECEIT **III**

THE BOSS MAN'S DAUGHTERS **III**

BAE BELONGS TO ME **II**

By **Aryanna**

TRUE SAVAGE **III**

By **Chris Green**

RAISED AS A GOON **III**

By **Ghost**

IF LOVING YOU IS WRONG…

By **Jelissa**

BLOODY COMMAS **II**

By **T.J. Edwards**

Available Now

(CLICK TO PURCHASE)

RESTRAINING ORDER **I & II**

By **CA$H & Coffee**

LOVE KNOWS NO BOUNDARIES **I II & III**

By **Coffee**

RAISED AS A GOON I & II

By **T.J.**

LAY IT DOWN **I & II**

LAST OF A DYING BREED

By **Jamaica**

LOYAL TO THE GAME

LOYAL TO THE GAME II

LOYAL TO THE GAME III

By **TJ & Jelissa**

PUSH IT TO THE LIMIT

By **Bre' Hayes**

BLOOD OF A BOSS **I II & III**

By **Askari**

THE STREETS BLEED MURDER **I, II & III**

THE HEART OF A GANGSTA

By **Jerry Jackson**

CUM FOR ME

CUM FOR ME 2

CUM FOR ME 3

An **LDP Erotica Collaboration**

BRIDE OF A HUSTLA **I & II**

THE FETTI GIRLS **I & II**

By **Destiny Skai**

WHEN A GOOD GIRL GOES BAD

By **Adrienne**

A GANGSTER'S REVENGE **I II III & IV**

THE BOSS MAN'S DAUGHTERS

THE BOSS MAN'S DAUGHTERS II

A SAVAGE LOVE **I & II**

BAE BELONGS TO ME

A HUSTLER'S DECEIT I, II

By **Aryanna**

A KINGPIN'S AMBITON

A KINGPIN'S AMBITION **II**

By **Ambitious**

TRUE SAVAGE

TRUE SAVAGE II

By **Chris Green**

A DOPEBOY'S PRAYER

By **Eddie "Wolf" Lee**

WHAT ABOUT US **I & II**

NEVER LOVE AGAIN

THUG ADDICTION

By **Kim Kaye**

THE KING CARTEL **I, II & III**

By **Frank Gresham**

THESE NIGGAS AIN'T LOYAL **I, II & III**

By **Nikki Tee**

GANGSTA SHYT **I II &III**

By **CATO**

THE ULTIMATE BETRAYAL

By **Phoenix**

BOSS'N UP **I & II**

By **Royal Nicole**

I LOVE YOU TO DEATH

By Destiny J

I RIDE FOR MY HITTA

I STILL RIDE FOR MY HITTA

By **Misty Holt**

LOVE & CHASIN' PAPER

By **Qay Crockett**

TO DIE IN VAIN

By **ASAD**

<u>BOOKS BY LDP'S CEO, CA$H</u>

(CLICK TO PURCHASE)

<u>TRUST IN NO MAN</u>

<u>TRUST IN NO MAN 2</u>

<u>TRUST IN NO MAN 3</u>

<u>BONDED BY BLOOD</u>

<u>SHORTY GOT A THUG</u>

<u>THUGS CRY</u>

<u>THUGS CRY 2</u>

<u>THUGS CRY 3</u>

<u>TRUST NO BITCH</u>

<u>TRUST NO BITCH 2</u>

<u>TRUST NO BITCH 3</u>

<u>TIL MY CASKET DROPS</u>

<u>RESTRAINING ORDER</u>

<u>RESTRAINING ORDER 2</u>

<u>IN LOVE WITH A CONVICT</u>

<u>Coming Soon</u>

BONDED BY BLOOD 2

BOW DOWN TO MY GANGSTA

T.J. Edwards